"Take off that ridiculous wig."

Without conscious thought Darcy did as she was told, her long golden hair flying about her shoulders as she whirled to see Lorenzo leaning nonchalantly against the mantelpiece. She suddenly felt sick with fright. "Y-you know...."

Lorenzo's dark eyes gleamed with cynical amusement. "My dear Darcy, I have always known that you were not Claire."

"But I don't understand," Darcy cried in bewilderment.

Lorenzo moved forward to pull her swiftly into his arms. "Your Great-Uncle Henry did not just go through the motions of a wedding rehearsal," he purred. "The good bishop has pronounced us man and wife—both in the sight of God and by law!"

His dark eyes stared intently down into hers and seared her mind, her very soul, with the terrible import of his message.

Books by Mary Lyons

HARLEQUIN PRESENTS

MARY LYONS

love's tangled web

Harlequin Books

TORONTO • NEW YORK • LONDON
AMSTERDAM • PARIS • SYDNEY • HAMBURG
STOCKHOLM • ATHENS • TOKYO • MILAN

Harlequin Presents first edition April 1985
ISBN 0-373-10779-X

Original hardcover edition published in 1984
by Mills & Boon Limited

CHAPTER ONE

THE late afternoon sun flowed in through the open casement windows, flickering over the bowed head of the tall, almost too finely drawn figure of a girl sitting in a chair, the glowing rays seeming to set alight the heavy curtain of rich golden hair which fell forward, masking her face.

Darcy put down her book with a sigh and leaning back, removed her heavy horn-rimmed spectacles, polishing them absent-mindedly as she gazed out of the window. Her wide blue eyes, the clear brilliant colour of lapis lazuli, swept blindly down the long avenue of lime trees, past the sheep grazing in the park and on to the distant salt marshes of the Suffolk coast.

What a fool you are! She told herself for the hundredth time that day. A complete and utter fool! It had been a great mistake to have listened to her mother's mad idea in the first place, and an even greater error to have allowed herself to be persuaded into taking part in this insane masquerade.

Sighing heavily, Darcy replaced her glasses and glanced down at her watch. Five o'clock. He would be here vey soon, and then what? She shivered with apprehension, dreading the thought of having to meet for the first time, the strange man who had arrived so unexpectedly two weeks ago. The stranger, who had not only bought their family home, but had also and simultaneously become engaged to her sister, Claire.

Jumping to her feet in agitation, she paced up and down the large bedroom. Trying to save the family bacon was one thing, but this scheme of her mother's— that she should impersonate Claire—was never going to work, not in a million years! If she, herself, had tried to dream up the ideal scenario for a guaranteed disaster, she could never have come up with anything more perfect than this crazy charade.

Going over to sit down wearily at her dressing table she began the difficult task of trying to stuff her long golden hair into a honey-blonde wig, the curls of which framed her face and fell down as far as her shoulders. Feeling almost sick with fright at the forthcoming encounter with her sister's fiancé, she couldn't help thinking with longing of her peaceful, academic life in Cambridge. She would have given everything she possessed to be safely there with her friend Sally in their small flat overlooking Midsummer Common, quietly working on her thesis.

She should have realised that something was wrong when her mother had telephoned her yesterday at the unearthly hour of seven o'clock in the morning. 'I must see you immediately. I'll be over as soon as I can,' Mrs Talbot commanded breathlessly, and rang off before Darcy had time to collect her sleepy wits.

She must have driven like Jehu to have covered the sixty-odd miles in such a short time, Darcy thought, opening her front door an hour and a half later to admit her mother's bustling, grey haired figure.

'Sally's just gone off to attend a lecture and I'm going to make some coffee. Do you want a cup?' she asked, leading her mother through the small sitting room into the kitchen. Her slim figure, clad in tight jeans topped by a baggy Aran sweater, had no trouble moving smoothly between the chairs and tables piled high with books. Not so her mother, who sighed with exasperation as her plump, rounded hips nudged against some heavy volumes which were impeding her progress.

'Really, darling. This place is such a mess,' she said, sitting down at the kitchen table.

'I know,' Darcy laughed. 'We were both working late last night, which is why,' she yawned, 'I need some coffee to wake me up before I set to and tackle the clearing up. Now,' she added, 'what's all this about? It's not like you to go charging around at this hour of the day.'

Mrs Talbot fiddled nervously with her handbag for a moment as her daughter placed the mugs of steaming coffee on the table and then sat down to face her.

'The fact is, Darcy,' she said, taking a deep breath and sitting up straight. 'Your father has managed to find someone to buy the Hall, at last. And ... and Claire's engaged to be married.'

'Heavens! Well, I mean, that's great news, isn't it?' Darcy took a sip of her coffee and looked at her mother. For the first time she noticed that the older woman's face looked unusually lined and unhappy. 'What's wrong? Is Father being very difficult about the sale?'

'No, not at all. In fact, dear, he is absolutely delighted.'

'*He's what?*' Darcy looked at her mother in amazement, remembering the battles fought by her mother to get Colonel Ralph Talbot to even consider selling the large rambling Elizabethan manor house which was the family home. It hadn't been until the bank threatened to foreclose that he had reluctantly and with much gnashing of teeth, agreed to put it on the market.

'Well, if Father's happy about the sale—incredible as it may seem—then what's the problem? Doesn't he approve of Claire's fiancé?'

'Oh, there's no question of your father not approving of your sister's engagement,' her mother smiled nervously. 'He fully approves. Well, it was his idea really, I suppose.'

'For goodness sake, Mother! The suspense is killing me. Who is Claire going to marry, and if Father is so pleased about everything, why are you looking so worried?'

Mrs Talbot sighed and faced her daughter resolutely.

'You see, Claire had been staying with some friends in London and suddenly returned home two weeks ago with this ... er ... this Italian. Actually, I think he comes from Sicily, but that's practically the same thing, isn't it?'

'Well, no, not really,' Darcy laughed. 'Still go on, I'm all ears.'

'As you know, your father's not ... er ... very keen on foreigners, but Claire persuaded him to show the man around the house after lunch and, well, the long and the short of it is that the ... the Sicilian offered to buy the house. For a great deal more than it is worth, I may say.'

'Hang on! Not only is Father against all foreigners, but he practically foams at the mouth on the subject of Italians! Didn't his eldest sister run off with an Italian fisherman? I never did find out the whole story.'

'Your Aunt Helen's elopement took place long before I married your father, Darcy, and I don't know the ins and outs of the affair, either. However, your father and this man got on very well indeed. He's ... er ... he's got a title,' she blushed slightly at the flash of cynicism in her daughter's eyes. 'His name's Lorenzo di Tancredi, Count Montreale.'

Darcy snorted in derision. 'Father's change of heart is now crystal clear—he always was a raving snob!'

'Oh, darling. You're always so hard on your father ...'

'For heaven's sake—what do you expect? He's always made it crystal clear that I'm a grievous disappointment to all his hopes for our family's future. Even when I managed to get a first class honours degree, all he could do was grumble about my not settling down and marrying a rich young man—preferably titled—who would rescue us all from dire poverty.' Darcy laughed harshly. 'All he cares about is that damn house of ours—and the family name, of course. We mustn't forget that, must we?' She shrugged dismissively. 'We've never got on, and it's a bit too late for either of us to change now. Anyway,' Darcy smiled, 'I'm still waiting for you to tell me what's gone wrong.'

'Well . . .' her mother paused. 'As you can imagine, your father didn't want to agree to the sale . . .'

'You're not going to tell me that Father turned this man down?' Darcy gasped incredulously. 'Not when the bank was threatening to call in his overdraft and loans, selling the house over his head? Not even Father could be so daft!'

Over the years her father had sold off all the land of what had once been a large estate, in order to finance various impractical get-rich-quick schemes, for all of which he was supremely unqualified. Darcy shuddered as she remembered the wine-making era when all the vines had died from some disease, and the experimental mink farm which was supposed to make their fortune. Thanks to a bite from one of the fierce beasts she still bore a scar on her hand to his day.

'No . . . Ralph didn't exactly turn the sale down . . .' Her mother paused, twisting her hands nervously in her lap. 'The truth is, Darcy, that he gave the . . . the Sicilian to understand that the Hall was tied up in some sort of family trust.' She looked unhappily down at the table. 'Your father said that if he wanted to buy the house, he would have to . . . er . . . to marry Claire.'

'For Heaven's sake!' Darcy laughed weakly. 'I don't believe it! I hope Claire had enough good sense to tell Father and this man where to get off. Besides which, I've never heard such a bare-faced lie. Honestly,' she shook her head ruefully, 'Father is the absolute limit—he really is!'

'Well, dear, I know that it's not strictly ethical . . .' Mrs Talbot sighed heavily. 'You're right, of course. It was an outright lie and I did speak very sternly to Ralph when he told me about it. But by then it was too late, you see.'

'No, I don't see. But I expect I shall in a minute. Go on.'

'Well, when your father told me about it, it was already a *fait accompli*. The Sicilian had accepted your father's terms and Claire seemed delighted with the idea. I promise you, Darcy,' she said earnestly. 'I did question her very closely as to whether she really wanted to marry this man Lorenzo, because the sale didn't have to go through if she didn't. However, she seemed very happy and delighted with the idea. She really did.'

'Look, I love my younger sister, you know I do, but she isn't known as "the dumb blonde" for nothing! She's sweet, but she can also be very silly. So I can see her possibly agreeing to Father's incredible proposal; though why this man would want to saddle himself with a wife as well as a large house, I can't for the life of me work out.'

'They must have known each other for a long time, and she just didn't tell us. Claire has lots of friends in London and often goes down to stay with them, as you know. She did seem very keen on an American boy at one time . . .' Mrs Talbot shrugged. 'However, there was absolutely no doubt that she was pleased to be engaged.'

'So—what's the problem?'

Her mother nervously tucked a strand of her grey hair back into the loose knot at the back of her head. 'The problem is that your father, having already received half the purchase price for the Hall, has gone mad and arranged a huge engagement party for tomorrow night. Everyone in the area's coming—absolutely everyone—plus half my family. And . . . and Claire's disappeared!'

'What do you mean, "disappeared"?' Darcy demanded with a worried frown.

'Well, after . . . er . . . getting unofficially engaged, Claire just mooched about the house for a few days, and then suddenly announced that she had to dash off to London. It wasn't until I went into her bedroom the next day that I found she had left me a note. Nothing very dramatic, just saying that she was going to be away for a few days and not to worry.'

'Well, that doesn't sound so terrible. Maybe she's staying in London with this Lorenzo chap?'

'No, she isn't. We haven't seen him since the day he bought the house, his lawyers have been handling everything. However, your father rang him up to invite him to the party—well, he's going to be the main guest, isn't he? So we had to check that the date was suitable for him. I can't tell you the frightful panic Ralph and I were in when he asked to speak to Claire! We managed to put him off by saying that she was out, but it doesn't solve the problem. Lorenzo's coming up tomorrow, arriving at tea time and expecting to see his new fiancée. What are we going to do if Claire isn't there?'

'Cancel the party, of course,' Darcy replied with brutal logic.

'Oh darling,' her mother wailed. 'We can't! It's far too late for one thing, and for another, your father's already paid the money he's received into the bank— they've been so pressing as you know. If Lorenzo finds that Claire's not there, he might . . .'

'. . . might think again about the deal?' her daughter completed the sentence. 'I don't suppose there's a chance of Father getting hold of the money to pay this Lorenzo back? No, I don't suppose there is,' she agreed as her mother shook her head dejectedly.

'Since the bank has waited so long for father to clear his loans and overdraft, I can see that it's a forlorn hope to think they'd let it go again. I suppose if you think about it,' Darcy added slowly, 'Father's guilty of some sort of fraud. I know he's got this overwhelming obsession about the family hanging on to the Hall and the continuation of the family name, but it looks as if he's tried to be a little too clever this time. I mean, I'm no lawyer, but it does seem as if he's taken this man's money under false pretences, doesn't it?'

'I've been so worried—you've no idea!' her mother assured her. 'And then last night I had this brilliant idea. One that could solve all our problems.'

'What idea?'

'Well, I was tossing and turning all night, and then it suddenly came to me in a flash! You must take Claire's place. Just for the evening, of course. What do you think?'

'What do I think?' Darcy gasped, looking at her mother in stunned horror. 'I think you're out of your mind—that's what I think!'

And nothing that had happened since had caused her to change her opinion, Darcy thought bitterly as the roar of a supercharged engine broke into her unhappy thoughts. She watched as a long, low black sports car snaked down the drive towards the Hall, sweeping around the gravelled forecourt and coming to rest by the heavy oak front door. Peering out of her window, all she could see was the far side of the vehicle as a small fat man got out and stretched his legs.

Ugh! He looks awful, she thought in dismay. I'm not surprised that Claire's run away. I wouldn't want to marry him, either. Still, she shrugged, it was no good putting off the inevitable confrontation. She'd better put in her contact lenses and then go downstairs; her mother would be up soon enough if she didn't.

There, that's done, she told herself a few moments later, dabbing at a stray tear in her wide blue eyes. The lenses which she so seldom wore were already making her eyes feel uncomfortable and gritty. It wouldn't do, she thought with a grim smile, for her sister's fiancé to find her in tears.

'For goodness sake, darling!' her mother burst into the room, panting and out of breath from having run up the stairs. 'Hurry up—he's arrived! Your father's keeping him busy downstairs at the moment, but he's already asked where you are . . .'

'Oh, stop fussing, Mother!' Darcy snapped irritably,

getting up from the dressing table. 'Oh dear,' she shrugged apologetically. 'I'm sorry to be so bad-tempered, but this whole mad, ghastly plan of yours is going to explode all over our faces like a rotten egg. I do wish I could get you to understand just what a ridiculous and preposterous scheme it is,' she added gloomily.

'Oh, darling, you did promise you'd go through with it . . .' Mrs Talbot looked at the unhappy figure of her daughter with a worried frown.

'Yes, I know I did—more fool me!' Darcy sighed heavily. 'It's all right, I gave you my word and I'll stick to it. But for God's sake don't blame me if this damned wig falls off or if some other disaster occurs, because no one but a fool—or you darling—would ever have dreamed up such an insane idea!'

Looking at her mother's anxious face, Darcy shrugged with weary resignation. 'I'll do my best, I promise. But since we none of us know anything about this man—who incidentally looks perfectly revolting—this afternoon's little tea party is going to be like tip-toeing through a minefield, isn't it? I could cheerfully strangle Claire, really I could.'

'I've made your father promise to take him off to look around the stables as soon as possible, and I'll step in and whip you upstairs if it looks as if something is going to go wrong. But really, dear,' she assured her daughter as they left the room, 'he's a very nice, friendly man.'

'Here we are, at last,' her mother sang out happily, if a little hysterically as she led the way into the oak panelled sitting room.

'*Buona Sera*, Claire.' Darcy gave a nervous start at the softly sibilant, faintly accented rich, dark voice of the man who rose as she entered the room.

Expecting to see the small, fat man she had viewed leaving the sports car, her eyes travelled with increasing incredulity up over the tall, broad shouldered and immensely powerful looking figure walking slowly towards her.

Hairs tingled nervously down the length of her spine, her confused mind registering deep shock at the sheer animal magnetism of the man who seemed to tower over her own five foot eight inches. Dark, blue-black eyes gleamed cynically down at her from beneath heavy eyelids edged with thick, curly lashes. They were, she thought distractedly, the only faintly feminine aspect in the otherwise hard-boned, rugged masculinity of the stranger's tanned face.

'How pretty you look. *Che carina—angelo mio!*' he murmured, looking down at his fiancée. Darcy stood gazing up at him, paralysed with fright, her eyelids blinking anxiously as she noted the unexpectedly sardonic tone in his voice.

She cleared her throat nervously. 'Oh ... hello, Lorenzo. I ... er ... I hope that you had a good journey down from ... from London. I mean ... I mean, I hope that the traffic wasn't too bad ...' she babbled helplessly as he took her hands and raised them towards his lips. A moment later his grip suddenly tightened, his powerful body stiffening into a sinister stillness.

Oh God! Something's wrong, she thought in panic, looking feverishly at his head of thick black hair streaked with silver, which completely masked the face bent over her fingers.

Her mind raced as she tried to sort through the available possibilities. She had remembered to wear Claire's usual perfume, so it couldn't be that. An engagement ring? Of course! He was sure to have given a ring to Claire ... She suddenly felt quite sick with apprehension and looked wildly at her mother, desperately trying to signal that a major problem had arisen. One that hadn't occurred to either of them.

Mrs Talbot gazed back at her daughter with a helpless shrug. Oh, well, I always knew it wouldn't work, Darcy thought with resignation. She could hardly pretend that she had already lost a ring which had supposedly only been on her sister's finger for two weeks. Her face flushed as she glanced fearfully up at the tall man, waiting for the storm to break over her head.

Lorenzo raised his head, subjecting her to a brief, searchingly intense and speculative look before his heavy eyelids descended, hiding all expression other than that of lazy amusement.

'You must forgive me, *cara*,' he said smoothly. 'I nearly forgot to present you with your engagement ring. Very remiss of me, wasn't it?'

Darcy nearly sagged with relief at his words, waiting submissively as he took a small box from his pocket. She couldn't prevent herself from giving a gasp of wonder as Lorenzo took her left hand and slid a huge diamond ring on to her finger.

'You mustn't look surprised, *cara*. It was your choice, surely? Although it would appear to be somewhat loose. Your finger must have shrunk during the last two weeks, humm?'

'Yes. Yes, I ... er ... I do seem to have lost a bit of weight, lately. I ... er ...'

'What a lovely ring, darling.' Mrs Talbot smiled and came forward to take Lorenzo's arm. 'You must come over here and sit down beside me, dear boy. There are so many things I want to talk to you about, and there will be plenty of time for you and Claire to catch up on each other's news later.'

'*Si, d'accordo, signora,*' he replied, flashing Darcy a sardonic grin as he obeyed her mother's summons.

Good old mother! The cavalry to the rescue in the nick of time, thought Darcy, staggering towards a sofa on legs which suddenly seemed to have turned to cotton wool. With nervous, trembling hands she accepted a cup of tea from her father, who was being unnaturally silent. As well he might be! she thought angrily. The whole ghastly business was all his damned fault in the first place.

She noticed that her mother was piling Lorenzo's plate high with thin cucumber sandwiches. That should keep him busy for a while anyway, she breathed with relief, looking carefully at the stranger who had suddenly descended into their midst.

She would have known immediately that he wasn't English. Instead of the usual grey flannels and checked sport coat, his tall, commanding figure wore a dove grey suit which forcibly displayed his wide shoulders and slim hips. His black hair, streaked with silver, was swept back like a lion's mane over a tanned autocratic face which contrasted sharply with his plain white silk shirt and dark tie.

Darcy felt far too frightened to do more than mutter monosyllabic answers to any conversation directed her way, intensely aware of Lorenzo's speculative gaze flicking over her silent figure as with nervous fingers she toyed with a piece of cake which she was quite unable to eat.

Watching as Lorenzo chatted so charmingly with her mother and father, Darcy shivered with fright. With every nerve in her body, every fibre of her being, she wanted to scream an urgent warning to alert her parents to their crass, blind stupidity. This man, so calmly sipping his tea, was certainly not the 'nice, friendly' character her mother blithely imagined. Neither was he a simple dupe to be taken in by one of her father's more nefarious schemes.

Hardly able to control her weak, trembling knees, she realised with despair that the expensive tailoring which clothed Lorenzo di Tancredi, Count Montreale's powerful frame, did little to sheathe his raw, vibrantly physical aura of controlled savagery. A restrained ferocity that boded ill for anyone so incredibly foolish as to even think of challenging his authority.

Mercifully her father, mindful of his instructions,

very soon suggested that Lorenzo should accompany
him to see over the stable block. Which was in far
better condition than the house, she thought grimly,
since Colonel Ralph Talbot had always preferred horses
to people. Lorenzo smilingly agreed to the scheme, sped
on his way by her mother's bright chatter about how
busy she and Claire were going to be getting the rooms
ready for the party later that night.

'But, surely it already looks perfect?' he murmured,
looking around the room and admiring the pedestal
flower arrangements and the gleaming furniture.

Darcy caught the dry, sardonic note in his voice, a
tone to which her parents seemed deaf, and for one
heart-stopping moment she feared that he was going to
insist that she accompany him. She tried to school her
face into a blank mask, but from the swift glance of
ironic amusement he sent in her direction, she wasn't
sure that she had succeeded.

As soon as Lorenzo and her father disappeared
through the french windows, Darcy leapt to her feet.
Ignoring her mother's delighted congratulations on her
success, she ran swiftly out of the room to seek
sanctuary in her bedroom. Sitting down at her dressing
table, she shuddered at the false reflection in the mirror
before reaching up to tear off the hateful honey-
coloured wig and allowing her own golden hair to fall
in a long, shining stream down her back.

Half an hour later, Darcy's stunned mind was still
trying to assimilate the magnitude of her father's
mistake. By trying to ensure that a Talbot—even a
female one—would continue to live at Belmont Hall,
not only was he possibly guilty of fraud, but he had at
the same time caught a tiger by the tail, and one that
was likely to give him a savage bite.

She had argued fiercely and long with her mother
that she was only Claire's sister, not her twin. That their
hair colouring was quite different from each other's, that
she was as blind as a bat without her glasses and to

crown it all, she was much slimmer and taller than Claire.

None of which sensible, logical objections, she realised with dismay, had made the slightest dent in her mother's blind adherence to an impossible scheme.

'Now simmer down, Darcy, and I'll deal with all the points you've raised,' Mrs Talbot had answered, calmly sipping her coffee in Darcy's flat yesterday. Was it really only yesterday? Darcy thought, shaking her head in bemusement.

'First of all, and possibly most important,' her mother continued inexorably, 'the guests at the party and Lorenzo too for that matter, will be expecting Claire. Unless something goes drastically wrong there is no reason for them to think otherwise. That's a tremendous advantage. Secondly, your voices are absolutely the same. You know that I always have to ask which of you is speaking on the phone.'

'Yes, but . . .'

'Claire's colouring is merely a toned down version of your own. You've always considered her so pretty, but you could be far more beautiful if you made even the slightest effort; which you don't.' Her mother looked disapprovingly at the long, heavy, rich golden hair scraped tightly back from Darcy's forehead and clasped by a thick, brown rubber band at her neck. She grimaced at the heavy horn-rimmed spectacles which always seemed to be slipping down the slim nose, giving her daughter a peculiarly owlish look.

Mrs Talbot sighed heavily. 'And why you have to look as if you get your clothes from Oxfam, I'll never know.'

'Oh Mother, I'm just not interested . . .'

'Well, you should be. You could be a lovely girl, instead of which you look a mess. However, I'm straying off the point. You'll have to wear a wig of course, but that's no problem. There's no need to cut and dye your hair just for the night.'

'Gee! Thanks,' Darcy muttered sarcastically.

'You'll have to wear your contact lenses,' her mother stated firmly. 'Unfortunately, we can't do much about you being thinner than Claire . . .'

'How about me pining away because I haven't seen him for two whole weeks?' Darcy joked in a biting voice, looking on helplessly as the older woman nodded enthusiastically.

'A very good point, Darcy. I'm glad to see that you're being helpful at last.'

'Oh, for Heaven's sake!' her daughter groaned in despair.

'As for your being taller—that's easily remedied. Flat shoes should take off those extra inches,' her mother announced triumphantly. 'There, I think that's taken care of everything.'

'Everything, except my agreeing to participate in this mad scheme! I . . . I can't possibly do it, Mother. Apart from the built-in disaster factor, which must be running at ninety-nine per cent; there's Richard. How in the world could I ever explain such a . . . a lunatic plan?'

'Why should he worry? You're not engaged to him yet. Mind you, the way you look, it's no wonder Richard hasn't named the day.'

'Now, just hang on a minute!' Darcy bridled. 'What's happened to the poor old mother who was moaning for my help a moment ago? As for when Richard Petrie and I get married—we'll do it in our own good time, if you don't mind. He's . . . well, he's tied up with his project in the Cavendish laboratory at the moment and far too busy to think of getting married. What's more, I've still got a year to go before I finish my thesis. There'll be plenty of time to think of marriage after that. Incidentally,' she added with heavy irony, 'I thought we were discussing Claire's problems, not mine?'

'Do you really love Richard?' her mother asked, disregarding Darcy's last pointed remark.

Darcy wriggled uncomfortably. 'Quite honestly, I'm not sure what anyone means when they say they're "in love". I mean, Richard's so terrifically clever, absolutely brilliant in fact. Some of the work he's doing at the moment—well, rumour has it that he could collect a Nobel Prize!' Her eyes shone enthusiastically. 'I know that he's a lot older than I am, but I do admire him enormously, and I ... I feel comfortable with him. That's enough, surely?'

Her mother sighed unhappily. Darcy's relationship with Richard Petrie, brilliant research chemist though he might be, sounded thoroughly unromantic. Still, she was only twenty-two and there was plenty of time for her to discover that there was more to love than admiring a man's brains.

In the end, of course, Darcy thought grimly as she went to run a bath, her mother had worn her resistance down to the point where she had agreed to take part in what she regarded as a deranged and disastrous project.

Removing her clothes, she caught a glimpse of her slim body in a full-length mirror and frowned, turning away hurriedly. That was another aspect of the whole terrible business, about which she had been quite unable to talk to her mother. She had absolutely no idea what sort of relationship Claire enjoyed with her fiancé. Italians were supposed to be hot-blooded weren't they? Claire was so pretty and vivacious that ... well, it was more than probable that they were lovers.

Darcy flushed unhappily as she lowered herself into the bath. The extent of her sexual experience had been abstracted, somewhat lukewarm kisses from Richard. It wasn't that he didn't care, she assured herself as she had done so often in the past, it was just that he had his mind on higher things. She, for her part, had been similarly preoccupied with her studies. It was only lately that she had found herself feeling so restless, so dissatisfied. Her mother's question yesterday had brought the matter firmly to the front of her mind.

Was she in love with Richard? How did anyone know, really know, whether they were in love or not? It's just that . . . she sighed despondently, it wasn't as if she wanted him to leap on her, or anything like that. The thought of Richard showing any highly-charged emotion was too extraordinary an idea to contemplate with any seriousness. While she knew that there must be more to life than a peck on the cheek, having read one or two torrid novels she wasn't at all sure that the sort of passion depicted between their pages would suit her at all.

Towelling herself dry, Darcy walked back into the bedroom gazing with apprehension at the dress which hung from her wardrobe door. On her reluctant acceptance of her mother's plan, Darcy had been speedily whisked off to an exclusive dress shop in Cambridge.

'That looks perfect,' Mrs Talbot had insisted over Darcy's muttered protests as an assistant produced a pale cream creation in silk organza and lace.

'Caroline Charles,' the saleswoman murmured, slipping the rustling material over Darcy's head. 'Pricey, of course, but so very romantic.'

'We'll take it,' her mother said decisively as scarcely recognising herself, Darcy had stared at her reflection with bemused wonder.

She had the same feeling of not being in touch with reality as she stood gazing now in the full-length mirror, at a girl she didn't know. It was like some secret fantasy come to life. The pale cream lace emphasised the soft tone of her skin as it caressed her shoulders, delicately revealing with sensual subtlety the rounded swell of her breasts in the low-cut neckline. The tight fitted bodice drew attention to her slim waist while the skirt, a floating cloud of lace embroidered silk organza, billowed about her as she turned reluctantly away from her new Cinderella self.

Darcy had just finished stuffing her long, thick hair

inside the curly wig, when there was a discreet knock and her mother slipped silently into the room.

'Do hurry, darling. Some of the guests have arrived already.'

'Oh God, how I hate this wig,' Darcy groaned unhappily. 'Can you check and see if there's any hair showing at the back?'

Her mother came over and made a small adjustment. 'There now, that's better.' She stepped back. 'You know, it's almost uncanny! You look so like Claire I can hardly believe it, and I must say again how pleased I am that everything went off so well at tea today. I'm so grateful, Darcy. I really am.'

'Well, I nearly had a heart attack over that business of the ring! It's awfully heavy and ... and I hate to wear it, somehow. It's ... well, it's Claire's, if you know what I mean.'

'Of course I do,' her mother put an arm about her slim shoulders. 'Now, you mustn't worry any more, we're practically home and dry. With so many people around, and having to act the good hostess, you'll easily be able to avoid getting too close to Lorenzo. He'll be leaving with everyone else of course, and then that will be that, thank goodness.'

'I've just got to put my lenses in,' Darcy removed her glasses and reached blindly forward for the little box. Her searching fingers brushed awkwardly against a jar of cream and knocked over the box which fell to the floor, spilling its contents on to the carpet.

Darcy slipped off the dressing stool, feeling through the carpet with desperate hands. 'Damn!' she muttered, 'that's all I need.'

'Leave it to me, darling,' her mother knelt down to help and Darcy got to her feet, stepping backwards out of her mother's way.

'I know we haven't much time to discuss it, but you really must warn Father very strongly about Lorenzo. He ... he's very dangerous and I'm frightened that ...

Oh God!' Darcy whispered in despair as she felt the crunch of glass beneath her thin evening slippers. 'What in the hell am I going to do?' she wailed. 'You know I'm as blind as a bat without my glasses. Two feet away from my nose and . . . and everything is just a blur!'

'Why, in Heaven's name, you can't have plastic lenses like everyone else, instead of those glass ones, I don't know,' her mother snapped irritably.

'Because they don't work on me—that's why,' Darcy cried. 'I . . . I tried some years ago, and I found them far too painful to wear for more than an hour or so.'

'Never mind, darling, what's done is done and there's no point in us having a row about it, is there?' her mother spoke soothingly. 'You'll just have to go downstairs as you are.'

'I . . . I can't,' Darcy gasped breathlessly, trembling with fright. 'You've simply got no idea of the problem. I mean, I . . . I can hardly see you now, and you're only about three feet away.' She leaned forward, touching her mother's shoulder. 'You see? I won't be able to walk across a room without bumping into someone, or see who I'm talking to or . . . or anything!'

Darcy's eyes filled with tears of helpless rage and frustration. 'As for avoiding Lorenzo,' she ground out through teeth that chattered with tension, 'There's not a hope in hell! How can I—when I won't be able to see him?'

CHAPTER TWO

FIVE minutes later Darcy, with trembling legs, walked slowly beside her mother towards the top of the stairs.

Mrs Talbot, while not minimising the problem, had pointed out to her daughter that she had no choice but to try and cope with the disastrous lack of contact lenses.

'There's no need to worry, darling. I promise not to leave your side all evening and I'll let you know well in advance exactly who you're going to meet. It will be all right, really it will.'

'It will have to be, won't it?' Darcy had groaned. 'For goodness sake just make sure that I get my hands on a stiff drink as soon as possible. I'm going to need all the help I can get!'

Now, as her foot moved carefully over and down the first of the wide oak stairs she was intensely grateful that she knew the house. The thought of trying to creep blindly around a strange place would be enough to scare anyone witless. Although, she thought wryly, that seemed a very fair description of how she felt at the moment.

'There's nobody in the hall except your father who is talking to Lorenzo and ... goodness me!' her mother whispered in surprise. 'Your great-uncle Henry has turned up. I can't think why your father had to go and invite him, of all people.'

'Let's hope the old Bishop's not as ga-ga as usual,' Darcy muttered, taking a deep breath and trying to remain calm at the thought of the ordeal ahead of her as she continued her slow, blind descent of the stairs.

'Claire, darling. How lovely you look tonight,' her father called happily, hurrying forward to take her hand and give her a kiss on the cheek.

His iron grey hair and beaming face materialised from the mist around her. *He's really incredible,* she thought in confusion. *If I didn't know better, I'd think that he truly believes that I'm Claire.* It suddenly occurred to her that since Colonel Ralph Talbot lived in some cloud-cuckoo land for most of his waking hours, he was quite capable of dismissing all problems and convincing himself that it really was his favourite daughter, Claire, who stood before him.

'Isn't your fiancée looking beautiful, Lorenzo?' The Colonel turned to the dark figure standing behind him.

Oh Father! she groaned inwardly as Lorenzo came forward, raising her nervous hands to his lips.

'Indeed. *Tu sei cosi bella, carissima.*' Once again she caught the faintly sardonic note in his deep drawling voice and instinctively raised her head in sharp defiance. Only to be cast into confusion by the gleam in his glittering dark eyes as they roamed with lazy insolence over her trembling figure.

Her cheeks flushed under his analytical appraisal. After the disastrous accident to her lenses upstairs she was already feeling upset, and it was with considerable difficulty that she conquered a sudden overwhelming urge to slap his handsome face.

You must keep your temper, she counselled herself desperately. This man is Claire's fiancé and she, poor fool, is supposed to love him. She seethed with frustration at not being able to give Lorenzo the sharp set-down that he so richly deserved.

'G-good evening, Lorenzo,' she managed to say at last, with some measure of calmness, hoping that he hadn't heard the stray note of asperity in her voice which she couldn't quite control.

She had no way of telling what Lorenzo's reactions were as he beckoned behind him. 'You must remember Wilkins, of course,' he murmured as the small, fat man she had seen getting out of the sports car earlier in the afternoon, swam into her sight, carrying a tray.

'Oh yes, yes of course,' she said, nodding in his direction.

Who on earth is Wilkins? she thought in bewilderment. Lorenzo offered no explanation and Wilkins she noticed said nothing as Lorenzo placed a firm arm about her waist. 'Come, my dear Claire. We must go and meet your parents' guests, yes?'

He smiled down into her lovely face. *A smile that doesn't quite reach those hard, dark eyes of his,* she thought, feeling frightened and stifled by the sheer height and breadth of his powerful figure.

Moving smoothly and adroitly, her mother stepped forward. 'Dear Lorenzo,' she murmured, smiling winsomely up into his tanned face. 'I'm sure you will forgive me if I just borrow Claire for a few moments. There are so many relatives she hasn't seen for such a long time, and I know that my husband wants to introduce you to some of your new neighbours. You do understand, don't you?'

For a moment, Darcy thought that his powerful body stiffened, but it must have been her imagination, she decided, as he gave a low laugh of amusement.

'Of course, *signora*. There will be plenty of time later on for my fiancée and I to further our relationship. Isn't that so, *carissima*?' he purred.

'Y-yes . . . L-Lorenzo . . .' Darcy stuttered breathlessly as his cool lips brushed her flushed cheek. The words and his silky expression sounded more like a threat than a promise, she thought in sudden panic.

'Thank God you rescued me,' she whispered, squeezing her mother's arm in thankful relief as they walked slowly away across the hall. 'Darling, I'm sorry, but I've simply got to have a drink. Heaven knows I'm going to need something to get me through this evening. Especially after an encounter with that ghastly man.'

'My dear, I think he looks very handsome. I can't think why you don't like him.'

'Like him!' Darcy squeaked incredulously. 'You and

Father—not to mention Claire—must be out of your tiny minds! I was trying to warn you upstairs, when I trod on the lenses. He's ... well, he's terrifying. I've never seen anyone who looks so dangerous,' she shivered nervously.

'Don't be silly, dear. He seems very nice and friendly.'

'For God's sake!' Darcy hissed out of the side of her mouth as she acknowledged with a brief smile the congratulations of a neighbouring farmer. 'I'm supposed to be the one who can't see! Why can't you and Father understand?' she continued, striving desperately to alert her mother to the frightening quicksands of any dealings with Lorenzo. 'He's like ... he's like one of those lions roaming around a safari park. As you've just said they look such "nice and friendly" beasts, don't they? But put one foot outside your car—and they'll have you for supper!'

Darcy tried to calm her trembling figure. 'I promise you, he'd be quite capable of murdering us all if he finds out what's going on. I simply can't understand how you managed to cook up this scheme, not when you must have already met and talked to him.'

Her mother patted her hand. 'Darling, you mustn't exaggerate so. It's just nerves, really it is. Here's James with a tray. You'll feel better once you've got a drink inside you.'

Shrugging helplessly at her inability to convey her warning, Darcy sighed heavily and accepted a glass of champagne.

'That's right, ducks. You get that down and you'll be all right in a mo.' The well-known, gravelly voice of James, ex-sergeant major in her father's regiment, now the family's general factotum and her very good friend, was followed by the appearance of his kindly face from the surrounding mist, gazing at her troubled expression with concern.

'Don't you worry, my girl. If that crafty sister of

yours turns up unexpected like, I'll make sure I grab hold of her and see she don't put no spoke in your wheel. By the by,' he added, turning to her mother. 'I've got that old geezer, the Bishop, in my snug. He's as happy as a lark, wrapped around a good bottle of port, so he won't be likely to cause any trouble.'

'That's a splendid idea, James. Well done!' Mrs Talbot smiled thankfully at him before turning to her daughter. 'Come on darling. We've got to go and meet everyone. It will look most peculiar if we don't.'

'Just make sure you keep Lorenzo as far away from me as possible,' Darcy shuddered. 'I can't stand him, he makes me feel so . . . so peculiar. And who,' she asked, struck by a sudden thought, 'who was that man Wilkins?'

'I don't really know, dear. Lorenzo refers to him as his valet, but he's been helping James with the drinks. So kind of Lorenzo to bring him to help, wasn't it?'

'Well, I think it's damn condescending of him,' Darcy muttered as they entered the drawing room.

'Hush,' her mother cautioned. 'Here's your aunt Cora and that frightful husband of hers. Hello darling. How lovely to see you,' she cried, embracing her sister. 'I know that you haven't seen Claire for ages.'

'No, we haven't, but we're going to be making up for lost time very soon!' Darcy's aunt laughed happily. 'We've just been asked by your father, Claire, if we'd allow our four darling grandchildren to be bridesmaids at your wedding. Wasn't it too sweet of Ralph to ask us? Of course, we said "yes" straight away.'

And the very best of luck to you, my dear sister, thought Darcy, trying to keep a straight face as she accepted her aunt's kiss. I wouldn't have those little horrors at my wedding—not if I was paid a million pounds! She knew she ought to be feeling sorry for Claire, who had been landed with such a large problem at her forthcoming marriage ceremony, but her chief feeling was that it served her sister right for having placed Darcy in her present intolerable situation.

As they progressed around the room greeting friends and relatives, it appeared that the Colonel had indeed been busy. He had already arranged for further young grandchildren on her mother's side of the family to act as pages at Claire's wedding, choosing with unerring accuracy the two who were far and away the worst behaved.

'Those boys will cause mayhem!' her mother gasped with ill-concealed horror. 'I'll have a word with you later, Ralph,' she hissed angrily, before she and Darcy were caught up again by old friends and neighbours anxious to confer their congratulations on the happy bride-to-be.

'This wig must be too tight,' Darcy muttered, smiling blindly at a complete stranger. 'I seem to have got a sort of buzzing in my ears. I really thought I heard music just now.'

'Oh Lord, I'd completely forgotten to tell you that your father has arranged for an orchestra to play during supper and for dancing afterwards.'

'He's mad! We can't possibly afford . . . Oh dear, yes we can afford it now, can't we? You know, I'll never get used to the thought that the family isn't on the bread-line any more.'

Darcy raised her wrist to her tired, strained blue eyes. She could hardly believe that only an hour had passed since she had walked down the oak staircase. She sighed with despondency at the thought of the long evening in front of her. Well, at least her second meeting with Lorenzo had gone off all right, thank goodness. Maybe she could develop a bad headache which would necessitate her having to retire to her room . . .

'Ah, *signora* . . .' She spun around as the dark, hateful voice of her sister's fiancé spoke behind her. Narrowing her eyes, she concentrated on trying to bring her short sighted vision to bear on the tall figure murmuring in her mother's ear. It was a waste of time, she realised, miserably aware that she had only her

clumsy self to blame for the destruction of the much
needed lenses.

'Oh my goodness—how awful!' her mother whispered
in distress. 'I'll be right back . . .' and before Darcy
could stop her, she had hurried away.

'What . . . what's happened?' Darcy asked nervously
as Lorenzo placed a firm hand on her arm, propelling
her slowly towards the french windows which opened
out on to the terrace and rose garden beyond.

'It is very unfortunate,' he murmured, not trying to
hide the amusement in his voice. 'It would appear that
the aged Bishop has consumed too much port!'

'I'm sure that I ought to go and help my mother,' she
said as firmly as she could. 'If you'll just excuse me . . .'
she paused, her heart sinking as she suddenly realised
that she wasn't able to see across the large room, let
alone find her way to the door without bumping into
some of the guests.

'There is absolutely no need to assist your mother. I
am sure that the situation is well under control by now.'
Lorenzo slipped a strong arm about her slender waist as
he led her out on to the terrace. 'Besides which,' he
added, 'it is surely right that we should have some time
together, yes?'

'Yes, I . . . I suppose so . . .' she muttered with
resignation as he led her across the stone paving slabs
towards a seat in a corner by the balustrade.

'You don't sound very enthusiastic, *cara*,' his dark
eyes gleamed down at her reluctant figure with dry
amusement.

'Oh yes, I . . . er . . . yes, I am. Really . . . very happy,
Lorenzo. Of course I am.' Darcy smiled as brightly as
she could up into his tanned face, trying to hide the
mounting panic she felt at being abandoned by her
mother and left alone with this terrifying man.

'*Va bene*. Let us sit down here and talk quietly,
hmm?'

She noted with dismay that his idea of sitting down

and talking quietly was very different from her own interpretation of the words. His arm still firmly encircled her waist, the faint elusive perfume of his aftershave mingling with his own musky, masculine scent teased her nostrils, and she found herself becoming almost shockingly aware of his raw, vibrant sexuality.

'Your father has been talking to me about our forthcoming wedding, my dear Claire . . .' He paused, looking down at her in the moonlight.

'Oh yes?' she murmured distractedly as he began drawing her closer to his dark suited figure.

'Yes. It seems that he is anxious that you should be married from your old ancestral home, and is therefore asking that our wedding date should be brought nearer than we had . . . er . . . anticipated. Since your parents will wish to begin packing up their furniture, etc., and I too wish to arrange for my builders and decorators to start work as soon as possible, it is perhaps a good idea, no?'

'No . . . I'm sorry . . . I mean yes, of course. I'm sure that it's a good idea . . . just fine . . .' Darcy answered breathlessly, confusedly losing the thread of what he was saying as her heart began to pound loudly in her breast.

'There will, of course, be much to arrange,' he gave a dry, sardonic laugh. 'Your mother has a very large family, has she not?'

'Yes, we . . . er . . . we sometimes joke that it seems like the twelve tribes of Israel,' she replied, trying to control her shaking hands. 'On my father's side of the family it is exactly the opposite. He has no living relatives and so there's only myself and . . .' she checked suddenly. 'Only myself and my sister, Darcy,' she added hurriedly.

Oh, for God's sake, come and rescue me soon, Mother! she prayed fervently. I'm going to blow the gaff any minute, I know I am.

'Ah yes, your sister. It is strange, surely, that she is not present this evening?' he purred, running a slim finger down her pale cheek.

'Yes, well . . . she couldn't make it tonight. She's . . . she's abroad,' Darcy improvised wildly. 'Yes, that's where she is—abroad.'

His hand slipped down to gently caress the soft hollows at the base of her neck. 'I see,' he murmured blandly. 'Just what . . . er . . . country is she visiting?'

'Oh . . . I . . . um . . . nowhere special. Just . . . just abroad,' she gasped, desperately trying to ignore his sensual touch. Her body began to tremble nervously and she found that, quite inexplicably, she was having considerable difficulty in breathing.

'Ah. Well, it would seem that we have satisfactorily disposed of your family, *cara*, including your sister who is . . . er . . . abroad.' The wry amused note in his voice changed as he placed a warm hand beneath her chin, tilting her face up towards him. 'Which just leaves the two of us out here, under the moon on this lovely evening, yes?'

His warm, seductive tones seemed to be affecting her rapidly beating heart in an alarming manner as he looked down at her, shaking his head sorrowfully. 'You are not being very loving towards me tonight, *angelo mio*.'

'I'm . . . I'm not?' she murmured, mesmerised by the gleaming dark eyes regarding her so intently.

'Alas no,' he sighed dramatically. 'Where are your passionate kisses? Your tender embrace?'

'My . . . my what?' she whispered in confusion as he put his strong arms about her quivering figure, drawing her closely to him.

'That is a matter we must rectify immediately,' he murmured as his dark head came down towards her.

'No . . . please . . . I . . .' She wasn't able to say any more, her protests cut short as his mouth possessed her trembling lips, teasing them apart with soft gentle kisses before his arms tightened, like bands of steel, moulding her firmly to the hard length of his muscular chest. His kiss deepened as he slowly began a sensual exploratory invasion of the inner softness of her mouth.

Darcy felt almost faint with dizziness, the blood in her veins seeming to leap, flaring into a molten flame at the unaccustomed sensations he was arousing. Her heart began to beat in an uneven, crazy rhythm, as his scorching lips and devastatingly experienced tongue compelled her to ardently and passionately respond to his lovemaking.

Helplessly enmeshed by a force she didn't recognise and couldn't possibly control, Darcy moaned beneath his passionate onslaught, her slim arms tightening about his neck, her fingers burying themselves convulsively in his thick, black hair.

Lorenzo's lips seemed to linger reluctantly as they left her mouth and trailed down to the wildly beating pulse at the base of her throat. He slowly raised his head, looking down at her with gleaming, enigmatic dark eyes.

Slowly surfacing from the deep mists of desire, Darcy felt as if she was returning from a journey to some far distant land as she pressed trembling fingers against her swollen, vulnerable lips. Her body shook as if in the grip of some raging fever from his kiss, the like of which she had never experienced before. It had swiftly shattered all her prosaic, childish illusions about the relationship between a man and a woman, and had awakened in her a pulsating fire that left her feeling helplessly weak and aching for fulfilment.

A moment later she blushed a deep crimson as she realised just how her treacherous body had betrayed not only her, but her sister. How could she possibly ever face Claire after what had happened? Or ... or Lorenzo, for that matter? She couldn't really blame him for what had taken place. He had, after all, merely indulged in what was, she supposed, his normal relationship with her sister. Oh Claire, she moaned silently, please forgive me . . .

Lorenzo watched with unfathomable eyes the various expressions chasing themselves across the flushed features of the girl who lay dazed in his arms. He took her hand, smiling gently as he kissed her fingers. 'It is possibly time for supper, yes? Shall we return to the party, *cara*?'

'Yes, yes please . . .' she whispered, thankful for the strength of his arm about her waist, without which she would have fallen as she tried to rise, her trembling legs seeming scarcely able to bear her weight.

'Are you all right, darling?' her mother asked, looking anxiously at her daughter's flushed face as they entered the drawing room.

'Yes, I'm fine . . .' Darcy murmured, quite unable to meet her eyes.

'I wonder, *signora*, if you will excuse me. I would just like to have a word with Wilkins for a moment.'

'Of course, Lorenzo. I think he's through there, in the library.' She watched as his tall figure strode away, and then turned to Darcy.

'I'm so terribly sorry to have left you in the lurch, like that. It was all a silly mistake. Poor old Uncle Henry was quite all right, drinking happily in James' snug. I can't think how dear Lorenzo came to get matters so muddled.'

Can't you? thought Darcy cynically. 'Dear Lorenzo' fully intended to have a lovemaking session with his fiancée and he had ruthlessly manipulated her mother and everyone else to achieve his desired purpose. I don't care if it wasn't really his fault, she told herself angrily. I hate him . . . hate him . . . the words thundered in her head as she seethed with a frustrated longing to hit back at the man who had shattered her innocent illusions. She couldn't possibly explain what had happened to her mother, even the very thought of doing so brought a flush to her cheeks.

'Are you sure you feel all right, darling?' Mrs Talbot looked at her perplexed.

'I'm okay. Just stop fussing,' she snapped, and then felt immediately contrite at taking out her general misery on her mother. 'Really, I'm fine,' she added in a softer tone. 'Let's go and have some supper and see if we can't think of a good excuse for me to disappear as soon as possible.'

Darcy hardly noticed what she ate. She helped herself blindly from the various dishes laid out on the buffet table in the large dining room, and then went to sit with some cousins to consume her meal. Since she knew them very well, she was able to hold her own in the general conversation, recognising a voice when she couldn't actually see the speaker's face. She felt shielded by their presence, finding it easier as the night went by to assume the character of Claire who was not known, thankfully, for making profound statements. Just as long as she participated briefly in the jokes and repartee, she felt safe. Especially since receiving her mother's whispered information that Lorenzo had been buttoned-holed by a local member of the National Trust. The person concerned felt strongly about the preservation of old buidings and Lorenzo was bound to be firmly trapped for the next hour, at least.

Darcy was therefore stunned and alarmed to hear the dark, rich voice that she was coming to hate, asking her to dance. She tried to refuse, but her companions pushed her to her feet with cries of encouragement.

'Come on Claire! It's not like you to be backward in coming forward. Not like that blue-stocking of a sister of yours—wouldn't catch her tripping the light fantastic!' one of her older cousins shouted, before he went off into peals of laughter.

I never did like him, she thought grimly. He was a horrid little boy and he obviously hasn't improved now he's grown up. She moved cautiously and tentatively forward, absurdly thankful, considering how she disliked him, to feel Lorenzo's firm hand grasp hers.

'I . . . I really don't feel like dancing,' she protested as he led her towards the large oak panelled music room, which was normally closed off, only being used for occasions such as this party.

'How can you say that, *cara*? Surely you can't have forgotten the nights we spent dancing together in London? You used to dance me off my feet,' he laughed sardonically down into her misty blue eyes.

'Yes, of course I remember . . . It's just . . . just that I'm feeling rather tired, that's all . . .' her voice trailed away as he propelled her inexorably into the dimly lit room.

'I really can't . . .' she muttered unhappily.

'Oh yes, *carissima*. Oh yes, you can,' he murmured, gently taking her into his arms, clasping her reluctant figure against the hard length of his body.

She felt hardly able to move, caught so closely to him as they swayed to the music that she was intimately aware of every muscle in his powerful frame.

Darcy tried desperately to ignore the sensations engendered by his cool cheek pressed so closely to hers, determinedly trying not to respond to the touch of his lips as they slowly trailed across her forehead and down over her temple. She was unable to prevent a violent shiver as his tongue gently and sensuously explored the outer shell of her ear before his mouth moved slowly to delicately sketch the outline of her lips.

'No . . . please Lorenzo. It's . . . it's wrong. I . . .'

'How can it be wrong, *cara*? We are to be married, yes?' he whispered as he covered her face in soft butterfly kisses.

No, we aren't, she wanted to scream. And then there was no time for coherent thought as she slipped under the powerful spell of his seductive mouth. As his kiss deepened, an answering flame stirred and then raged through her trembling figure. Helplessly, and mindless of the innocent invitation, she moved her body erotically against him provoking a low groan deep in his throat as his hands began an experienced and practised exploration of her soft body. His fingers slid sensuously over the thin silk organza, Darcy moaning softly as his hand firmly possessed the warm, full curve of her breast.

It took them both some moments to realise that the band had stopped playing. Darcy's cheeks flamed with mortification at her inexcusable behaviour and she prayed fervently that the dim lighting would hide the guilty blushes she could feel suffusing her face. What could she possibly say, or do? She had never felt so ashamed of herself as she did at this moment, leaning against the linenfold panelling of the music room walls for support, and trying to look anywhere other than into the face of the man who towered above her.

It would seem ludicrous to try and explain, even if she could—and clearly she couldn't—that this was the first time she had allowed any man to touch her as he had done. Let alone the way he had . . . had kissed her, she tortured herself. What in the world had come over her, that she could behave so loosely and so disgracefully with her sister's fiancé?

Tears welled in her eyes and her lips quivered in remorse as she acknowledged that not only had she behaved badly, but she didn't even like the man. In fact, she feared and hated him. She closed her eyes tightly to prevent the tears from falling as she fought to control her emotions.

The hooded eyes regarding her so intently, narrowed fractionally as they glimpsed her obvious distress. Lorenzo cleared his throat huskily. 'I think it is time that we both had a drink, yes?'

She nodded unhappily and allowed him to lead her through to the bar set up in the morning room.

'Champagne, Lorenzo?' her mother called, approaching with James who carried a large tray.

'Thank you,' he replied, handing a glass to Darcy and taking one himself. 'To you, my dear future mother-in-law,' he smiled, toasting her mother. 'It has been a charming evening and how sad that it has to end.'

'Yes, isn't it,' agreed Mrs Talbot, happily tossing back the sparkling liquid and smiling broadly at the approaching end of what had been an exhausting evening. One, however, that appeared to be crowned with the successful accomplishment of her eldest daughter's masquerade.

'What a pity that we didn't arrange for you to spend the rest of the weekend here with us, Lorenzo,' she added with careless relief. 'However, you must come and stay with us before we have to leave the Hall.'

'Ah, my dear *signora*. There is, surely, no time like the present? I am delighted to accept your very kind invitation and will be very pleased to stay the night.'

'What?' she cried, her control slipping for a moment as she regarded her future son-in-law with consternation. 'I mean . . . I mean you haven't brought a case with you or . . . or anything,' she protested, trying to make a brave recovery from her shocked response to his words.

'There is absolutely no need to worry. Unless, of course, there are no spare bedrooms in such a large house?' he murmured sardonically. 'I could possibly use the one I changed in?'

'No . . . I mean . . . yes, of course we have plenty of spare bedrooms. That is . . .'

With mounting dismay, Darcy watched her mother floundering helplessly beneath Lorenzo's charming bland smile.

'I know you'll forgive me,' he confessed with a disarming grin, 'but I was hoping that you would invite me to stay the night. So I despatched Wilkins in my car to London, two hours ago. It won't take him long to pack my things and return, the roads are clear at this time of night. So kind of you to ask me,' he added, raising Mrs Talbot's hand to his lips.

Even without her glasses, Darcy was quite able to see that despite his soft, blandishing words, the dark glittering eyes beneath those heavy lids held a careful, watchful expression as they flicked swiftly between her mother and herself.

'Yes, well, I'm delighted that you can . . . er . . . stay with us . . .' her mother sagged unhappily.

'My dear *signora*, what can be wrong? You don't look at all well. I'll just go and get you another glass of champagne.'

Darcy was almost sure that she caught a note of amusement in his bland voice as he turned and walked away.

Left on their own, mother and daughter looked at each other in dawning horror. 'I told you that bloody man was dangerous, didn't I?' Darcy hissed angrily. 'As soon as I set my short-sighted eyes on him, even I knew he was trouble with a capital "T".'

'But he doesn't suspect anything, darling. Surely not?'

'No . . . no I'm sure he doesn't, not if his . . . his behaviour is anything to go by!' Darcy retorted grimly. 'However, I've had it. I'm absolutely whacked, not to say totally exhausted. I really can't take another moment of this ghastly farce, so if you'll lead me to the bottom of the stairs, I'm going to bed—and to hell with everyone!'

'But darling,' her mother whispered as she led her from the room. 'What on earth are we going to do?'

'I don't know, and at the moment I don't care very much one way or the other,' Darcy muttered as she stumbled up the first steps of the staircase. 'I've decided that like Scarlet O'Hara, I'll think about it tomorrow!'

CHAPTER THREE

AFTER a disturbed night in which she had tossed and turned incessantly, Darcy woke up the next morning feeling sluggish and depressed. She put out a hand to her bedside table, sighing with relief as her fingers encountered her horn-rimmed spectacles.

Thank God for the ability to see! Her eyes still felt tired and sore from the strain of trying so hard last night to focus on people and objects, most of whom were far beyond her normal range of vision.

Putting on her glasses, she lay back on the pillows and stared at the top of her four poster bed as other memories of last night's party came stealing insidiously into her mind. A brilliant tide of colour swept across Darcy's pale cheeks as she recollected with horrific clarity every detail of her encounters with Lorenzo.

How could she? How could she have responded to his kisses so . . . well, the way she had? Surely she could have stopped him from pursuing his experienced love-making? she accused herself bitterly.

Sighing deeply, she pushed a distraught hand through her long gold hair. How could she have repulsed him without giving the game away? Lorenzo and Claire obviously had a . . . well, a passionate and . . . er . . . ardent relationship. Any objection, any withdrawal on her part would have been sure to have aroused his suspicions.

I don't know who I'm trying to fool, she thought miserably. It was quite clear that Lorenzo had only to put his lips to hers and she had been putty in his hands. Hands . . .! Darcy turned over, burying her flaming face in the pillows as she tried to shut her mind and body to the recollection of exactly how she had moaned with pleasure at his experienced touch.

She had never . . . Not even with Richard had she . . . The thought of Richard Petrie behaving in such a passionate way brought a hysterical bubble to her throat. She supposed that a heart did beat somewhere beneath the hairy, woollen checked shirts Richard normally wore. However, he would be far more likely to ascribe her present feelings, the throbbing ache in the pit of her stomach for instance, to a change in the chemical formula of her body!

Darcy immediately felt guilty at such disloyal thoughts and sat up in bed, pushing aside the blankets. She wasn't going to achieve anything by lying here feeling ashamed and sorry for herself. She had to do some constructive thinking, particularly about how she and her mother were going to avoid Lorenzo's continuing presence. In order to do that, she had to have a cup of coffee to help wake her up.

Snatching up her dressing gown and putting on her slippers, she moved across the room. With her hand on the old iron latch she hesitated, wondering if it was safe to leave her room without wearing the wig. A glance at her bedside clock showed that it was only eight o'clock. Who had ever heard of guests waking that early, and especially after a party? Feeling quite secure, she slipped along the top landing and down the back staircase to the kitchen.

Warming her hands on the ancient and temperamental Aga cooker while she waited for the kettle to boil, Darcy looked out of the lead lined, diamond panes of the large kitchen window. The early morning sun shone out of a clear blue sky, giving every promise of a perfect summer's day. How on earth, she wondered, was she going to be able to avoid Lorenzo. The only resource left open to her would seem to be that of a sudden and wildly infectious disease, she thought grimly.

''Ullo, 'ullo! You're looking a bit down in the dumps, Darcy,' James' hoarse grating voice broke through her reverie as he came into the kitchen carrying a hod of

coke for the Aga. 'You didn't ought to be down here
without that wig, you know,' he added warningly.

'I know,' she sighed, as he riddled and then emptied
the hod into the old stove. 'Whew!' she wrinkled her
nose at a cloud of dust which rose and settled on the
old copper pans hanging on the walls. 'That cooker's
just about had it,' she added, sneezing as the smoke
tickled her nostrils.

'Well, that foreign chap can put in a new one, it's not
our problem any more, is it?' James replied with a
shrug. 'By the way. How are you planning to get rid of
him? Your ma and I had a bit of a chat last night, and
we're stumped.'

'We all are,' she groaned, the mounting pressures of
the difficult day ahead seeming to lie like a heavy
burden on her shoulders.

'Mind you, that bloke Wilkins is all right. Him and
his wife, she does the housekeeping apparently, they live
in the foreigner's place in London. Very posh it is, so he
said. Got what he called "a panoramic view" of
London, it has.'

'I don't suppose you managed to find how long
they're staying?' she queried hopefully.

James shook his head. 'No. Sorry, Darcy. It wasn't for
lack of trying, but he didn't know either. This place is
getting to be like an hotel, isn't it?' he grumbled. 'Mind
you, after I'd given him a few stiff drinks he did let slip a
few things. He was dead surprised to be told to go back to
London and get his boss's clothes. He calls him "contay"
by the way.' He gave a sniff of disapproval.

'Oh James!' Darcy laughed. 'You sound just like
Father! "*conte*" is only the Italian version of count, the
same as one of our earls, I suppose.'

'La-de-da foreigners,' he mumbled, making himself a
pot of tea. 'Anyway, that chap Wilkins had to cancel
some business meetings today. I ask you, who does
business on a Saturday?'

'I don't know, James. It's not my sort of thing.'

'Yeah, well, it ain't mine an' all. Another thing that Wilkins said . . .' James hesitated for a moment. 'Well, I wouldn't tell your sister, of course. But it looks like her fiancé's a regular one for the women, if you know what I mean?'

'Yes,' Darcy's lips tightened grimly. 'Yes, I bet he is!'

'Still, we've got to think positive, Darcy. That sister of yours, Claire, she's going to be living like Lady Muck, isn't she? His Nibs' lifestyle all sounds a bit grand for the likes of us. What with me just helping out here, and Mrs Harding coming up from the village to do the cleaning. I dunno, I'm not used to all these grand goings on.'

'Neither am I, James,' she sighed wearily. 'However, I must get back upstairs before I'm spotted.'

Back in her bedroom, Darcy went over to sit by the window, her brow creased with thought. She and her mother had been so preoccupied in organising the substitution of Darcy for Claire, that she for her part had hardly given any thought to Lorenzo. What sort of man was it who came to lunch and within an hour had decided to buy the house?

Why Belmont Hall, of all places? she thought perplexed. Built of rose red brick, the Elizabethan manor house looked today much as it must have been at the time it was built by one of her ancestors. The façade of two outer gables and a smaller central one forming the letter 'E', was typical of many built in the latter days of Good Queen Bess' reign, and subsequent generations of the family had hardly altered the original house in any way. To an historian it might well appear to be an architectural gem, but to anyone of even the most limited sense, it was quite clearly a most uncomfortable house.

On a lovely summer's day like this one, it was delightful as the sun shone on the leaded panes and the mellow red brick. However, such halcyon days were few and far between. The east wind, whose biting force felt as if it came all the way from the steppes of Russia, had always and unerringly found its way through the joins in the stone mullioned windows. Electrictity had only been put in after the last war, and there was no heating system other than the huge fireplaces.

Darcy's chief memories of her childhood were those she had spent huddled over small log fires set in the large stone grates, her blue hands covered with chilblains. She and Claire had coined a joke. Question: How do you get dressed on a winter's morning? Answer: Very quickly!

So, what reason could there be for a Sicilian Count to want to buy such a large and inconvenient house in the depths of Suffolk? It wasn't for retirement purposes because he simply didn't look old enough—he couldn't be more than forty at the most. However, he had got engaged to Claire, so he must be intending to settle down here. Although from the look of him, she thought sourly, the fleshpots of London were far more his scene.

She was still sitting baffled at not being able to find any satisfactory answers to her questions, when her mother slipped into the room.

'Oh Darcy, isn't it awful!' She sank down into a low chair. 'I've racked my brains all night and I can't think of any way of getting rid of Lorenzo; short of murdering him, that is.'

'Why can't I be suddenly taken ill? You know—flu or something equally drastic.'

'I thought of that immediately after you'd gone to bed, but that ghastly man spiked my guns. I suggested that you hadn't been looking very well lately, and do you know,' she looked at her daughter indignantly, 'Lorenzo merely remarked that he thought you looked fine. That after a good night's sleep you would be feeling much better, and that if you weren't well enough to get up in the morning, he'd come upstairs and look after his "beloved fiancée" himself!'

Mrs Talbot sighed unhappily. 'After that, I rather

gave up trying to think of good excuses. I should have listened to what you said. You were quite right all along. He's a dreadful man and very bad mannered to have taken me up so quickly on what was only a polite invitation for the future.'

'It wasn't bad manners,' Darcy said slowly. 'Well, not in the way you mean. He had every intention of staying the night and he just took the opportunity of your careless remark to clinch the matter. He would have found some other excuse, like his car breaking down, if you hadn't given him the perfect opening.'

'How peculiar. Are you sure?'

'Yes, I'm quite sure, although for the life of me I can't think why.'

'Well, the mattress in his bedroom is shockingly uncomfortable, full of lumps. I hope he didn't sleep a wink all night,' her mother said venomously.

Darcy laughed weakly. 'Oh Mother, we'll have to do better than that if we want to get rid of him, we really will. I can't go downstairs in these glasses, and there's no way I can hide my bad eyesight for the whole day. How long is he staying, by the way?'

'God knows,' the older woman replied gloomily. 'For weeks, at this rate, I should imagine. However, I've solved the problem of the glasses, I think.'

'How?' Darcy demanded eagerly.

'I suddenly remembered that the last time you were home you left your dark glasses behind. They're made up to your prescription and it is a sunny day after all.'

'Oh great! It may be a nice day, but how much sun do we get indoors? It won't work.'

'Oh yes it will. I've thought it all out and our story will be that you've got a hangover. You didn't eat much tea, which is why the champagne yesterday evening went straight to your head. On top of that, you didn't sleep a wink last night . . .'

'The only bit of truth in this whole farrago of nonsense,' Darcy interjected bitterly.

'So,' her mother concluded triumphantly, 'you have a hangover and need to wear dark glasses. All right?'

'I can't think why you aren't writing fiction, Mother! You'd have no problem thinking up plots, would you?' she retorted, suddenly feeling overwhelmed by a heavy weight of depression at being once more firmly enmeshed in the tangled threads of the masquerade.

Darcy spent the rest of the morning in her room, having arranged with her mother that she would not go downstairs until just before lunch. 'There's no point in courting disaster a moment before I need to,' she had said grimly.

The only disturbance in an otherwise peaceful morning, had been the sudden clattering roar of an engine in the sky, just as she finished dressing. Rushing to the window she had stared out with shocked amazement to see a helicopter landing on a lawn by the avenue of lime trees.

'For Heaven's sake!' she gasped as her mother came into the room. 'What's going on?'

'God knows! This place is becoming a madhouse.' Mrs Talbot put down the cup of coffee she had brought up to Darcy, and sank into a chair.

'Honestly, darling. I don't know whether I'm on my head or my heels. First of all that man of Lorenzo's—Wilkins—has completely taken over the kitchen. He's preparing lunch for us all and, would you believe it, teaching James how to make a white sauce!'

'You're kidding?'

'No I'm not, they've become the best of friends,' she gestured wearily. 'Frankly dear, Wilkins seems to be a far better cook than I am, so I decided to leave them both to it. What else could I do?'

'Nothing, I suppose.' Darcy shrugged and turned back to look out of the window. 'But . . . what's that helicopter doing here?'

'It belongs to Lorenzo—of course! He informed me with that wolfish smile of his that he knew I'd understand if his "aide" as he called him, flew up this morning, and could he borrow the library until lunchtime?'

'That must have been something else he fixed up last night,' Darcy looked at her mother in dismay.

'Well, darling, what could I do? I couldn't say no, could I? Anyway, you'll be glad to hear that the helicopter, his "aide" and Wilkins will be returning to London at lunchtime, apparently.'

'Is Lorenzo going as well?' Darcy asked with a sudden surge of hopeful release.

'No such luck,' her mother groaned. 'I think that he's intending to leave this evening, but it looks as if we've got him for the rest of the day. Drat the man!'

Darcy withdrew her head from the window and walked slowly over to a chair. 'I'm seriously worried Mother, about what this family's getting itself into. For Heaven's sake wake up and look at what's going on. You may be preoccupied with Claire's absence, but what sort of man is Lorenzo? What do you really know about him?'

'Well, dear . . . he's obviously very rich, of course.'

'And . . .?'

'Well . . .' her mother paused, looking at her daughter with a worried frown.

'Exactly! You don't know a blind thing about him, do you? You don't know whether he comes from Italy or Sicily; or why he should want to buy this house and bury himself in the depths of Suffolk. And just look at his lifestyle! Who do we know that carts a valet around with them, even supposing they employed such a rareified creature? And now we've got this helicopter on the lawn outside. Not exactly a normal way of life, is it?'

'I suppose he's a business man . . .'

'But you don't *know* do you? You know nothing about him, not even what sort of family he's got. I gather from James, who pumped Wilkins last night, that he's quite a womaniser. Has he been married before?'

'Darling, I . . . I don't know . . .' her mother moaned.

'Well, you'd better find out, and fast!' Darcy said forcibly. 'You can't just let poor Claire wander into marriage with this man without making sure that everything's above board. For all we know he could be a master criminal or something!'

'Darcy!' Mrs Talbot looked at her with shocked eyes. 'You can't really think . . .'

'No,' she sighed. 'I don't. But he's obviously as rich as Croesus and far and away above our touch. We may live in a large old house, but that's as far as it goes. You, of all people, must know we've never had two pennies to rub together. I can understand the lack of money that would make Father and you leap at Lorenzo's offer, but for goodness sake stop being so blind. You must try and find out who he is, and why he wants to buy this house when he'll obviously have to spend a fortune doing it up. Believe me, the whole thing doesn't make sense.'

She might have saved her breath, Darcy told herself with resignation as she sat silently at the lunch table. Despite the grim warning she had issued this morning, she watched in dismay as her mother and father fell willing victims to Lorenzo's overwhelming charm. How could they be so foolish? she raged inwardly, looking with loathing at Lorenzo's handsome face from behind the safety of her dark glasses.

She had been standing in the drawing room just before lunch, a stiff drink firmly clutched in her hand, when he had issued from the library. Once again she felt the shock engendered by his powerful presence as he strode across the room to her side. Wilkins has done a good job, she thought acidly, viewing his slim, hip-hugging beige slacks topped by a short-sleeved cream silk shirt, which was stretched tightly across his broad shoulders and open at the neck to display the strong column of his throat.

Darcy felt her knees beginning to knock against each other as he bent forward to kiss her lightly on the cheek.

'Ah *cara*. Your mother tells me that you are . . . er . . . not feeling very well.'

'N-no I'm not,' she said as firmly as she could, hating him afresh for the tone of sardonic amusement in his voice.

'The result of too much champagne, I understand.' He raised an eyebrow in cynical mockery. 'The one glass I saw you drinking must have gone a very long way indeed, yes?'

The damn man—he must have eyes in the back of his head. 'Oh well, you know how it is,' she shrugged coolly, trying to control her shaking hands as he gave a deep rumble of dry laughter.

'Oh yes, *cara*, I know exactly how it is!'

Darcy eyed him warily, not at all sure that he was referring to her hangover. But what else could he mean? Her thoughts were interrupted by the arrival of her mother and the noise of the helicopter taking off.

'Ah, *signora*. It was so very kind of you to allow me to complete my urgent business. I can't thank you enough for being so understanding.'

And that was that, Darcy thought, jabbing at her lemon souffl with an angry spoon. The way her mother had flushed as he raised her hands to his lips, not to mention the soft, caressing tone of his voice as he chatted to both her father and mother throughout lunch, had left her parents in a state of bemusement. He can charm the birds off the trees, she thought in fury, but he's certainly not going to get any change out of me!

'That was a wonderful lunch. So kind of you to let your Mr Wilkins cook it for us, Lorenzo,' her mother said with what Darcy thought caustically was a simpering smile.

'My pleasure,' he murmured as her father passed him

the brandy decanter, which he declined with a smile. 'I wonder if I might just look over the house again this afternoon,' he asked diffidently.

Darcy's head jerked up, all her instincts immediately on the alert. That soft, hesitant note wasn't his usual tone of voice, of that she was absolutely certain.

'Of course dear boy. By all means,' the Colonel replied expansively. 'Claire would love to show you around, wouldn't you dear?'

Oh no! she thought with a sinking heart. Even her father couldn't be that stupid. Her mother was nodding happily too—what was wrong with them both?

'Well, I don't think . . .'

'Nonsense,' her father said roundly. 'You can take Lorenzo around the park too, while you're at it. The fresh air will do you good.'

'*Va bene.*' Lorenzo's voice was studiously bland as he rose from his chair, although Darcy was well aware of the faint tinge of mockery in his dark, gleaming eyes as he looked at her across the table. 'Shall we go, *cara*?' he purred silkily.

If she hadn't been feeling so frightened, Darcy would have laughed at the dawning look of consternation on her mother's face as she realised, far too late, just how cleverly she and Colonel Talbot had been out-manoeuvered.

'Where . . . I mean, what would you like to see,' she asked nervously as they left the dining room.

'I am quite happy to leave it to you, my darling,' he drawled smoothly. His soft, sensuous tone caused shivers of apprehension to race down the length of her spine as he firmly took her hand in his.

Come on, pull yourself together, she told herself desperately. Her legs suddenly felt as weak as water at the disturbing gleam in his dark eyes, and she would have given everything she possessed to be able to sink down into one of the chairs beside her.

'You have been very . . . er . . . instructive,' he said

with a dry bark of laughter as they finished their tour at the minstrel's gallery overlooking the hall.

'Thank you, Lorenzo,' she murmured primly, her eyes dancing with malicious glee behind her dark glasses. If he hadn't been bored to death, it certainly wasn't her fault, she thought with satisfaction. There was nothing of the house's history, architecture, paintings or furniture which had escaped her attention as she had pointed out every minute and exhaustive detail.

'There is just one thing which you seem to have missed,' he murmured softly as she prepared to lead the way down the stairs.

'I can't think . . . Oh!' She turned to look at the large painting which was engaging his attention. Pride comes before a fall, she told herself miserably retracing her steps with leaden feet.

'It is of your sister and yourself, is it not?' He turned his dark head to look at her with sardonic amusement. 'I am surprised that you did not show this to me, hmm?'

Thankful that her sun glasses hid her consternation, she schooled her mouth into a careless smile. 'Yes. We were much younger then of course. It was painted the year my father won some money on the Derby. One of the few times he ever managed to back a winner,' she added bitterly.

She and Claire had been portrayed sitting with their arms around each other's waists, the house and park in the background. Their two heads were touching each other, and while it was not a particularly good likeness of Claire, the young painter had caught Darcy's amused expression very well. He had been particularly keen, she remembered, on displaying her long golden hair which flowed down over her shoulders.

'Your sister is very beautiful,' Lorenzo said slowly. 'Yes, very beautiful indeed.' He turned to look at her stiff, nervous figure.

'Well, she certainly doesn't think so,' she answered carelessly. 'Shall we go downstairs?'

'Of course,' he smiled and took her hand. 'Tell me,' he said, 'are you alike in your characters as well?'

'Good gracious no!' She gave an involuntary laugh before she remembered the role she had to play. 'No, my sister Darcy is ... well, I'm sure she won't mind me saying so, but she's really very boring. She lives buried in Cambridge and does nothing but read books all day. An absolute bluestocking—you wouldn't like her at all,' she added as defiantly as she could.

'Ah no, *cara*. I must love all your family, must I not? I look forward to meeting this sister of yours when she returns from ... er ... abroad. Perhaps at our wedding, yes?'

'That's not at all likely,' she replied firmly as she led the way out into the garden. 'My sister never goes anywhere—she's a recluse in fact. Far too busy trying to write her thesis to bother with things like weddings.'

Oh God! I wish we could get off the subject of 'me' she thought with a sinking heart as she realised that she was treading on very thin ice indeed.

'You are not being very kind about your sister, my darling. Only two weeks ago you were telling me how clever she was to have gained a scholarship to Cambridge and to have achieved a first class honours degree.' He slipped a strong arm about her slender waist, shaking his head sorrowfully.

'Now, you say she is "boring". On what subject does this boring sister of yours write her ... er ... thesis?' he queried with a soft laugh, catching her free hand and raising it to his lips, kissing each finger slowly.

Once again, as had happened last night, she suddenly felt breathless and confused at his proximity. The touch of his firm mouth as it lingered over her hand made her heart start beating uncomfortably.

'The Normans,' she gasped helplessly, mesmerised by the gleam in his dark eyes. 'The Expansion of the

Norman Empire in the South of Europe. I ... er ... I think that's what she's writing about,' she added hurriedly.

'How very interesting,' he said, letting go of her hand, although he still kept a firm arm about her slim waist. 'That was a Norman castle, was it not?' Lorenzo pointed to a tall, round ruined stone building on a grass covered mound across the park.

'Yes. That was built by the original owner of this estate, Richard Talbot who came from D'arcy in France. He accompanied William the Conqueror, as I'm sure my father has told you,' she added cynically.

'He seems very proud of his ancestry,' Lorenzo agreed. 'He tells me that it is very rare for there to be a descent in a direct line from father to son from that time until now.'

'Yes,' Darcy said bitterly. 'Father's practically demented on the subject. I ... er ... my sister Darcy, that is, studies history, but even she thinks he's far too obsessed about the subject. Anyway, it doesn't matter any more, since Father only has two daughters and nobody to carry on the family name.'

'I should like to see your Norman castle,' he said as they walked slowly across the lawn. 'I come from Sicily, as you know, and my ancestors were also Norman.'

'I did wonder, the name Tancredi is interesting. There was a Norman king of Sicily called Tancred. I ...' Darcy checked in sudden horror at having nearly given herself away. '... so ... so my sister told me. I ... I mean, it is unusual ... um ... not ... not English ...' She cursed inwardly at not being able to think of anything to cover up her mistake.

'Names can be confusing,' he agreed blandly, apparently not noticing her confusion. 'I am still puzzled by your sister's name, *cara*. And even more by the fact that it is apparently your name too.' He paused to let her through a gate which led to the small rise on which the ruin stood.

She really couldn't stand much more of this, she thought grimly. 'I . . . er . . . I told you that my father is obsessed with the family history. Not that he need be,' she added caustically. 'My ancestors lived here very quietly, keeping their heads down and not getting involved with any wars, civil or otherwise. In fact, they were a very sensible lot who just farmed their land and kept themselves well away from affairs of State.'

She paused, collecting her thoughts and determined not to make another gaffe. 'My father was determined to keep the family Christian name of "Darcy" going at all costs, despite the fact that he had no sons, only daughters. His name is Ralph, but his eldest brother who was killed in the war was called Darcy,' she explained. 'So, he insisted on having both I and my sister christened with the name. I . . . my older sister was unlucky in that the name stuck to her. As far as . . . er . . . I'm concerned, my mother went on strike and insisted in calling me Claire, despite my baptism certificate. Father's crazy of course,' she shrugged.

'Ah, now all is explained,' Lorenzo said as they stood outside the ruin. 'My home, in Sicily, is an old Norman castle. So you will see why I am so interested in an English one.' He smiled down at her. 'Not that I live there, of course. I have been living in London for some years and only go back when on holiday. My—or should I say our—home will now be here, *cara*. Yes?'

'Er . . . yes,' she murmured, as he led her inside the old ruin. 'It's not very interesting. There's only one room left intact and . . . it's very dark . . . and . . .' As if it were someone else, she could hear her breathless voice stumbling over the words as he led her inside the round keep, whose only light came from the sunlight shining through the arrow slits in the wall.

'It is not so very dark,' he said softly, looking around him. 'Although, of course, these are unnecessary,' he added, swiftly removing her dark glasses.

'Oh no! Please . . .' she muttered, looking blindly in his

direction. 'I really must keep them on, I can't . . . I can't . . .'

'You will not need them, for the next few minutes at least,' he murmured, putting his arms about her and drawing her towards him.

The light, mocking note in his voice was acutely disturbing, as was the strength of his embrace. Her body began to shake as she stood gazing up at the dark face above her, finding it impossible to glance away from his wide mouth which was curved into a sensual smile.

The amused gleam in his glinting dark eyes suddenly altered, their expression changing into one her inexperienced mind didn't recognise, but which provoked an instinctive trembling in her already nervous figure. Unconsciously she swayed towards him as his head came down towards her, driven by a force that banished all sense and caution.

His lips brushed hers, tenderly sketching the outline of her mouth with tantalisingly soft kisses, as light as butterfly's wings, before he pulled her roughly to him, his mouth closing possessively over hers.

Darcy felt as though she was drowning, sinking into some unfathomably deep pool beneath the rampant sensuality of his lips. A pulsing flame of desire flared into life and raged through her body as his kiss deepened, and she clutched at him blindly for support, responding ardently and passionately to the invasive mastery of his tongue.

She gave a small moan of disappointment as his mouth left hers to trail slowly down her arched neck, shivers of delight dancing across her skin as his lips found the hollows at the base of her throat.

'Si bella, bella carissima,' he murmured thickly, gently caressing the warm swell of her breasts. There was no thought of denying him as his fingers sought and found the buttons of her dress. Bewitched, gasping with delight, she leant back arching her body against his strong arm and crying out as his mouth closed over the swollen rosy tip which he had exposed to his view.

The sound of her cry in the enclosed space of the small room sent shock waves echoing and spiralling through her brain, forcing the hard, harsh light of reality to sear through her mind with startling clarity.

'Oh God!' she cried, struggling fiercely in his arms. 'Let me go ... Oh please ... I ...' she begged as he held her firmly against him, gently soothing her trembling figure.

'Hush, *carissima. Stai ferma.* Keep still, my darling. All is well—we are to be married soon, yes?'

'No ...!' she moaned as she leant weakly against his firm, hard chest. For one mad, insane moment she savoured the strength of his encircling arms, his warm, musky masculine scent, the total security of his embrace; before she blushed a deep crimson at such a treacherous, wicked abandonment. This was her sister's fiancé!

'Oh yes,' he said huskily as he began fastening her buttons. 'Oh yes, we will be married very soon, I promise you.'

CHAPTER FOUR

'OH, what a tangled web we weave, When first we practise to deceive!' The words from Sir Walter Scott's *Marmion*, which she had studied at school, echoed with an incessant, rhythmic beat in Darcy's aching head as she drove from Cambridge towards Belmont Hall.

'You're a stupid, weak fool,' she railed aloud, stamping her foot hard down on the accelerator in a spasm of anger at her own folly. 'Of all the silly . . .' She glanced down at the speedometer and saw with dismay that she was not only exceeding the speed limit, but was asking of her little second-hand car more than it could be expected to perform.

Simmer down, she told herself. Something that was easier to say than to do. It was five days since she had escaped from her family home for the peace and quiet of Cambridge. Unfortunately she hadn't been able to do any work on her thesis, finding it almost impossible to concentrate on anything, let alone her academic studies. Moreover, she seemed to be feeling sick with nerves all the time, and quite unable to face any food.

After their passionate interlude in the castle ruin, her silent, trembling figure had accompanied Lorenzo back to the house on feet that felt as heavy as lead. They found her mother and father having tea as they had entered the drawing room, and Darcy had sat in miserable silence as her parents and Lorenzo discussed the details of her sister's wedding.

With dazed eyes she had watched her mother's look of horror as her father announced that he had arranged for Mrs Talbot's uncle Henry to officiate at Claire's marriage.

'Got it all tied up last night,' he announced. 'Good

thing to have a member of the family officiating, what? The old boy was delighted to be asked and he agreed with me that the chapel here in the house would be perfect.' Colonel Talbot sat back in his chair with the satisfied smile of one who knows he has done his family duty.

'For Heaven's sake, Ralph!' her mother had protested angrily.

'Nothing wrong with the fellow, Olivia. Nothing at all. Can't think why you don't approve. He's a bishop, isn't he? He'll do very well for Claire. Can't see any problem myself.'

You wouldn't! Darcy thought grimly. Despite her own troubles she felt very sorry for Claire as she listened to her mother trying to explain the problem to Lorenzo.

'Ralph's quite right, of course. Henry's retired now, but he was one of the Anglican bishops in Africa: Togoland, I think it was. It's just ... well, how can I put it ...' she hesitated, trying to find words to explain her uncle's eccentricities to her daughter's fiancé.

'He's completely ga-ga. Absolutely round the bend,' Darcy found herself saying as she reluctantly came to her mother's rescue. 'Never knows where he is from one moment to the next. Or what he's doing for that matter. Honestly Father, surely you can remember what happened at our confirmation? That was another of your brilliant schemes, wasn't it?' she snapped angrily.

'Now, there's no need to ...'

'Yes there is! He thought it was a christening, didn't he? Getting him away from the font was a hell of a job which I can still remember vividly, even if you can't. I've never been so embarrassed in my life!'

'Well, it's too late now, because I've asked him and he's accepted,' Colonel Talbot replied mulishly. 'The chapel is licensed for weddings and I've already fixed it with the vicar chappie in the village. Lorenzo, here, has agreed to the date in three weeks' time, and that's that.'

'If you're insisting on having that idiot officiating at the wedding, you'll need a rehearsal to make sure he knows what he's supposed to be doing!' she retorted furiously as the mutual antagonism between her father and herself flared up between them.

'What an excellent idea!' The softly spoken words cut through the tense silence as father and daughter glared at each other. Darcy recovered herself first, glancing quickly at Lorenzo's bland, sardonic smile as he lounged back in his chair, his long legs stretched out before him.

'I . . . I didn't really mean . . .'

'But yes, *cara*. It is a very good suggestion. We do not want anything to go wrong with our . . . er . . . marriage, do we?' She blushed furiously beneath his glance of cynical amusement.

He turned to the Colonel. 'I have many business commitments between now and the wedding, but I can manage to attend such a rehearsal next week, if such a thing can be arranged in time?'

'Yes, of course. No trouble at all. In fact, a damn good idea, what?'

Father will think it's his own idea any minute now, Darcy thought, irritated at how easily Lorenzo was able to wrap her parents around his little finger. However, Claire was bound to be home by then and the rehearsal would at least help to make sure that her mother's eccentric uncle didn't make a pig's ear of the whole business. Poor Claire, she had thought with a sudden pang of sympathy. I wouldn't be in her shoes for anything.

And that, Darcy gave a bitter laugh as she drove towards her home, that has to be the joke of the year! Because that's exactly where she was—in Claire's shoes once again.

Her mother had phoned in desperation last night. Claire was still missing and Darcy must come and walk through the rehearsal in her place, *she must*!

Despite her spirited protests, she had known in her heart that she couldn't let her mother or her sister down. Her only bargaining counter being that she had extracted a promise that her mother would start telephoning the hospitals and notify the police immediately.

The only bright spot of the whole ghastly day so far, she mused as she turned into the long drive leading down to Belmont Hall, was that she had managed to find an old pair of contact lenses, they were far too weak, of course, but at least they were better than nothing.

There seemed to be far too many cars outside the house, she thought, having difficulty in finding a place to park. Glancing swiftly in her driving mirror to check that the wig was set straight on her hair, she took a deep breath and opened the car door.

'Darling!' her mother called as she walked into the house. 'Thank God you've come. I've told everyone that Claire has been out shopping. I don't know whether I'm coming or going, I really don't. You've no idea what your father's been organising. He's arranged for all the bridesmaids and pages to be here as well—it's absolute bedlam! I'm having to lay on some sort of lunch for everyone, of course. Well, we can't drag the children's parents over here and not feed them, can we?'

'Not those ghastly children?' Darcy looked at her mother in horror.

'Yes,' Mrs Talbot sighed. 'And they're far worse than I ever imagined. By the way,' she added in a whisper. 'I've already telephoned all the major London hospitals and none of them have anyone answering to Claire's name or description. I've also been in touch with the local police who are coming later today to take the details, although they don't think there is much they can do. There hasn't been a crime, you see.'

'Just make sure that you keep Father well away from me, or they'll be investigating a case of patricide!'

Darcy hissed as the hall began to fill up with chattering relatives. 'Whatever possessed him to ask those frightful kids?'

'Poor Claire,' her mother moaned softly in agreement.

'At the moment I'm far more concerned with "poor Darcy",' she retorted as her head began to throb angrily. 'Where's Lorenzo, by the way? I suppose it was too much to hope that he'd have a fatal accident on the way here?'

'Darcy!' her mother whispered in shocked tones. 'How can you say that?'

'Very easily!' she snapped. 'I take it that he's arrived?'

'Yes darling. He's in the library with Uncle Henry. They seem to be getting on very well, which is something I suppose,' she added wearily.

'Oh well—let's get on with this ... this charade,' Darcy groaned as her father, accompanied by Lorenzo and the bishop, came into the hall.

'Good morning, *cara*.' Lorenzo strode across the hall to her side. 'It would seem to be ... er ... busy here this morning, yes?'

'Oh, hello ...' she replied breathlessly, trying to ignore the way her pulse began to quicken as he slipped an arm about her waist. She couldn't prevent herself from giving an involuntary start as he trailed a tanned finger down her pale cheek, which flushed beneath his touch.

'Are you ready for our ... er ... marriage?' he drawled softly, gently brushing his lips across her trembling mouth.

'Please ...' she whispered desperately, her heart beating a savage tattoo. Surely he must be able to hear its loud, rapid thud?

'You mustn't be shy, my darling. It is our wedding, is it not?'

'No, it's not,' she muttered, provoked almost beyond measure by his overwhelming aura of raw masculinity, coupled with the cynical mockery evident in the dark hooded eyes gleaming down at her.

'It's only a rehearsal and . . . and don't you forget it!' Darcy glared at him, simply not caring any more whether she was stepping outside the character of Claire. Let him think what he liked—she'd had it!

Lorenzo's dark eyes merely flickered with lazy amusement, his lips curving into a ruthless smile.

'I see that the good bishop is ready, *cara*,' he murmured blandly. 'Your father is indicating that I must go and take my place. *Ciao, mia sposa!*' He bent to swiftly kiss her lips before walking lithely away.

'I'm not your damned wife—and neither am I going to be—thank God!' she muttered in fury after his departing figure.

Her father approached, rubbing his hands together complacently. 'Everything seems to be going off very well, I think. That musical cousin of yours has agreed to play for the wedding. He tells me we may have to get the instrument tuned somehow, but he's willing to give it a try today.'

'For Heaven's sake! I thought we were only supposed to be going roughly through the motions, just to make sure that Great Uncle Henry's got the right service for a change?' she looked at her father in dismay.

'Thought I'd take the opportunity to get the whole thing tickety-boo, what?' Colonel Talbot looked about him in annoyance. 'Where's your mother? I sent her off for a tablecloth well over five minutes ago. I can't think what she can have been doing.'

Darcy put a weary hand to her brow, wincing at the throbbing intensity of her headache. 'A tablecloth? Either I'm going mad or you are,' she groaned.

'Got to make sure those boys—the pages—know how to carry your bridal train, haven't we? Really! I seem to be the only person capable of organising anything around here! Ah, there you are Olivia. And about time too.'

'I'm sorry, Ralph,' her mother said. 'There's just been so much to organise . . .'

'Never mind that now,' her father barked. 'Tie that cloth around the girl and then we can get on with the job.'

'This whole thing's getting completely out of control,' Darcy moaned miserably as her mother bent down to knot the two ends around her daughter's waist. 'I feel such a fool,' she wailed.

'Come on you children. Line up in twos,' her father commanded. 'You boys at the front—that's right. Now take hold of that tablecloth . . . don't jerk it like that, you scrubby monster!' he shouted at one of the small boys, who merely grinned evilly back at him.

'Maybe asking that child to be a page was a mistake,' he muttered, taking his daughter's arm.

That has to be the understatement of the year, Darcy thought grimly, her heart sinking as she heard the strains of the Wedding March issuing from the chapel.

'Here we go then,' her father announced, leading the procession through the music room and down the steps into the family chapel.

As she had explained to Lorenzo during their tour of the house last weekend, the chapel was the only part of the original medieval manor house to have survived the Tudor rebuilding scheme undertaken by an ancestor. It had been refurnished since that time, of course, but Darcy never ceased to be stirred, as now, by the simple beauty of the small chapel. The sun streamed in through the stained glass windows set in Gothic arches behind the plain altar, falling on the old flag stones as she and her father moved slowly down the aisle.

'What's he dressed up like that for?' she whispered to her father in bewilderment, as her great-uncle entered the chapel from the small vestry in a white cape over long purple robes, and wearing a bishop's mitre on his head.

'Fellow looks quite as he ought. Taking it seriously

too—quite right. I knew you were wrong about the old boy,' her father barked, looking about him to make sure that everyone was in their place.

Darcy, who found herself standing beside Lorenzo, glanced quickly up through her eyelashes at his tall, commanding figure. He was looking down at her with a searchingly intense gaze that was far removed from his usual expression of sardonic amusement. Her face flushed a deep red as she hung her head, confused by the serious and determined stare from beneath his heavy lids.

'*Dearly beloved, we are gathered together here in the sight of God . . .*' The bishop's voice boomed around the small chapel.

Oh Claire, where are you? Darcy moaned silently. It was quite wrong somehow, that she should be standing here like this. Even a wedding rehearsal should be taken seriously and this . . . this charade suddenly seemed to be making a mockery of what should be an important part of Claire's life.

I can't . . . I really can't go on pretending like this, she thought confusedly as the majestic words of the 'service filled her ears, striking home the awful truth; that it was totally and absolutely wrong to deceive Lorenzo like this. I . . . I must tell him . . . I must stop this farce now. Maybe he'll understand that it wasn't really fraud on Father's part . . .

'. . . *If either of you know any impediment why you should not be lawfully joined together . . .*'

Darcy braced herself resolutely. Feeling sick with apprehension she took a deep breath and opened her mouth to explain exactly why the service should not continue.

The words had no chance to leave her throat as Lorenzo grasped her wrist tightly with his large hand, the fingers of which seemed to be made of steel as they bit into her flesh. Gasping with pain, she turned to look at him with incredulity as he smiled grimly down into her atonished blue eyes, lifting her hand still trapped in his firm grip towards his mouth.

'Please! You're hurting me,' she gasped, as his lips brushed over her fingers, before slowly releasing her hand.

What in the hell does he think he's doing? she thought angrily as she tried to rub some circulation back into her wrist which had been so forcibly seized. Kissing her hand in public like that! It was quite ridiculous and . . . and embarrassing as well.

Lorenzo was promising to love, comfort and honour her sister, when the tablecloth tied around her waist was tugged so hard as to nearly pull her backwards off her feet.

'What's going on?' she turned to find that the two pages were having a tug of war with the length of linen attached so firmly to her figure.

'Stop it at once,' she whispered angrily, grabbing one of the small boys by the shoulder. Nudged by her father, she turned back briefly to respond, 'I will,' to her great-uncle Henry's request that she should love, honour and obey Lorenzo. He'd be lucky! she thought with a flash of malice.

How Claire could contemplate the . . . 'Ow! You little beast!' she shouted as the child she was still holding firmly, sank his teeth into her hand, wriggled out of her grip and hit one of the small little girls acting as a bridesmaid.

Lorenzo whirled swiftly, grasping the boy by the scruff of the neck and administering a sharp blow to his rear, before scooping up the girl who was sobbing quietly and holding her comfortingly in his arms.

'Continue, my Lord Bishop,' he commanded as Great-Uncle Henry looked up in astonishment at the disturbed and milling group of people before him.

Darcy watched in bemusement as Lorenzo promised to take Darcy Talbot for his wedded wife. Standing beside Darcy, the little girl cuddled in his arms, he smiled calmly down into her confused face. Her blue eyes widened as she saw for the first time something of the man behind the usually cynical, sardonic mask. Her lips parted softly as she watched his solicitous and tender care of the small child.

'I, Darcy, take thee Lorenzo . . .' She stumbled over the words, her voice sounding as if it belonged to someone else. Pull yourself together, she told herself desperately. The Darcy referred to wasn't her, it was Claire's real name as well. This whole, miserable farce would be over soon and then perhaps she could find an opportunity to tell Lorenzo the truth. It wasn't fair to him, it really wasn't, she thought with a guilty pang.

Where . . . where did he find that ring? Her mind was in a whirl of total confusion as Lorenzo pushed the gold circle on to her finger. The ache in her head began to throb more fiercely than ever as the bishop droned on.

'. . . pronounce that they be man and wife together.' The words seemed to come from a long way off as she swayed wearily, the longing to put her head down in a cool dark room becoming almost more than she could resist.

'Oh no!' she moaned as the Bishop began yet another prayer.

'Have patience, cara, it will all be over very soon,' Lorenzo whispered softly. He put down the little girl who scampered happily back to join her sisters, as he slipped a comfortingly strong arm about Darcy's shoulders.

It was only because she wasn't feeling very well, and for no other reason, she told herself, that she allowed him to draw her tired, nervous figure to lean against his hard frame. For a few moments she relaxed and closed her eyes, savouring the feel of his soft mohair suit against her flushed cheek, the warm masculine smell of his after-shave.

The organ suddenly thundered into life and she

hastily straightened her figure, blushing deeply as she looked straight ahead at the altar.

'Thank goodness that's over. We can ... er ... we can go now, can't we?' she muttered looking about her as Lorenzo tucked her arm into his and led the way—not down the aisle, but following Great-Uncle Henry into the vestry.

'What ... what are we doing in here?' She gazed in bewilderment up into his tanned face and then turned as she heard her mother call her name across the small room.

Mrs Talbot bustled up, a broad smile on her face as she drew Darcy aside. 'Darling, isn't it wonderful,' she whispered with excitement as she helped untie the tablecloth. 'Claire has turned up—at last!'

'Really?' Darcy gasped, not able to believe that her nightmare had ended. 'Where is she?'

'I rushed her upstairs to your room and told her to wait there.' She hugged her daughter happily, her grin reflecting Darcy's own as they both realised that there would be no more need for subterfuge.

'I must go and see her immediately. She can put on this dress, even if it's a tight fit, and then take over,' Darcy babbled happily. 'Oh thank God, Mother. I'm so ... so ...' She shook her head, almost unable to express her overwhelming relief at being released from the strain of the last week.

'*Un attimo, cara!* Just a minute.' Lorenzo's deep voice caused her to pause in her hurried flight from the small vestry. He took her reluctant hand and drew her over to a small table. 'Your uncle asks that you should sign your name here,' he said, handing her a pen.

'How stupid—whatever for?' she muttered, doing as he asked, her mind racing busily over all the points she must make to Claire before her sister met Lorenzo again. For instance, she must tell her about the fact that she, Darcy, was supposed to be abroad and not able to come to the wedding.

'There,' she said, putting down the pen and giving Lorenzo a beaming smile of relief before she hurried from the room, pushing her way through the ranks of milling relatives as she rushed towards her bedroom.

'Claire? It really is you—*Oh thank God!*' Darcy leant for support against the closed door of her room as she gazed across at the mirror image of her present self.

Her sister who had been leaning out of the window, withdrew her head and smiled broadly. 'My goodness! I'd never have believed that you could look so like me. It must have been great fun . . .'

'*Fun!*' Darcy stared at her in amazement. 'You . . . you've absolutely no idea of just how ghastly it's been. Absolute hell, in fact. Where in Heaven's name have you been?' she demanded fiercely.

'Oh Darcy. I'm sorry, I really am,' her sister looked at her contritely. 'I . . . well, I wouldn't have gone away if it hadn't been so terribly important to me. I'm so happy—you've no idea. I'm going to get married and . . . and it's all so wonderful!' Claire laughed happily, dancing over to fall in a giggling heap on the bed.

'God save us!' Darcy muttered, staggering across the room on legs that had suddenly become as weak as water. Sinking down into a chair she found herself unable to stop her knees from shaking at the release of the strain and torment of the past week.

'I know you're getting married to Lorenzo, you idiot!' her voice grated roughly. 'What do you think I've been going around in this frightful wig for? Do pull yourself together and tell me what you've been doing,' she pleaded.

'Oh Darcy, don't be silly! I'm not going to marry old Lorenzo.'

'*What?*'

'Of course I'm not.' Claire beamed at her happily. 'I'm going to marry darling Roddy, and . . . Hey! Are you all right?' She looked with concern at her sister who was gazing at her with blank, dazed eyes, the blood seeming to drain away from a face that was already pale with strain.

'W-hat do you mean . . .?' Darcy breathed in horror, completely unable to comprehend her sister's words. 'Of course . . . of course you're going to marry Lorenzo. I . . . I've just gone through the most awful rehearsal for your wedding. How can you possibly say that you're not going to marry him . . .?' She jumped to her feet gesticulating wildly in an effort to make her sister understand.

'Don't be silly! You can't have thought that I'd go along with such a mad scheme of Father's? I'm not that daft, you know!' Claire laughed. 'Still, it did prod darling Roddy into asking me to marry him, and . . .'

'Who in the hell is "darling Roddy"?' Darcy demanded grimly.

'Roderick Lovell III. He's . . . he's wonderful, Darcy, he really is. I love him so much.' Claire gazed mistily at her sister. 'We met when he was working in London for the Chase Manhattan Bank, but then he had to go back to New York and I was really heartbroken, you've no idea how miserable I was. And . . . and then he rang me up and proposed. Well, of course I accepted and I've just come back from America . . .'

'America?' Darcy shook her head in dazed confusion. 'What on earth were you doing in America? I'm sorry Claire, it's . . . well, it all seems to be so . . . so . . .' she shrugged helplessly.

'I went over to meet Roddy's parents of course. They practically own Boston and I wasn't sure that they'd approve of me, but they were so sweet and kind. They think I'm a perfect English Rose!' she added smugly.

'Oh, for God's sake . . .'

'I'll tell you something else,' Claire confided, 'you know all that stuff that Father forced down our throats—about the family being so old and all that rubbish? Well, you wouldn't believe how well it went down in Boston! Amazing isn't it?'

'I . . . I can't cope with any of this,' Darcy moaned, pausing as she was struck by a sudden thought. 'How in the world did you manage to afford the fare to America? It must have cost a fortune to fly there and back at such short notice.'

'Honestly! You're always so practical, Darcy. I don't think you've got a romantic bone in your body,' Claire muttered, her cheeks flushing slightly. 'If . . . if you must know, a . . . a friend paid for the trip. It was by Concorde, and a really fantastic flight, so fast and comfortable. Anyway,' she added hurriedly, 'I'm much more concerned about how Father and Mother will react to the news. I do want them to approve of Roddy—what do you think?'

What do I think! Darcy checked suddenly, listening with dismay to her scream of exasperation echoing around the room. Sinking down on to the chair, she buried her head in her hands, almost unable to face the problems which lay ahead.

'Claire,' she said at last, taking a deep breath and trying to speak reasonably to her sister, who was regarding her with a fatuously happy grin. 'Can't you see that it's just not a simple matter of "goodbye Lorenzo" and "hello Roddy"—I only wish it were! You must . . . you really must understand what's happened while you've been away. Lorenzo accepted Father's deal and has paid the money for the house—well half of it anyway. Father isn't in a position to return the money and . . . and . . .' she shrugged unhappily. 'Surely Claire, even you can see that it leaves us in a dreadful position if you now decide you don't want to marry Lorenzo. I . . . well, I rather think that Father has been guilty of fraud, although I'm not entirely sure.'

'It's no good going on, Darcy. I'm madly in love with Roddy and I can't help it if Father has been silly again, can I? Anyway, there's no problem. Lorenzo will get the house if he's paid the money as you say, and if Father has been made to look a fool, well, that's just too bad!'

'Too bad, is right—you frightful girl!' Darcy raged.
'When I think what I've had to put up with from . . .
from your damned fiancé! I simply don't understand
how you can just throw him over so casually? Especially
after . . . well, after the sort of relationship you must
have had. Not that I blame you,' she added grimly.
'The man's a bloody sex-maniac!'

Claire laughed. 'What relationship? You are being
silly, you know. I've never even kissed Lorenzo,
although I suppose he did peck me on the cheek when
we got engaged. I promise you, Darcy,' she looked
earnestly at her sister, 'you've no need to worry—none
at all. I mean, he's very nice of course, but he's not my
type at all. Really he isn't.'

Darcy sat looking at Claire in stunned silence. There
was no denying the patent honesty in her voice. So . . .
so what had been going on? Her head throbbed as her
bewildered mind simply refused to cope with any more
shocks after the battering it had received lately.

'Oh my God!' she said suddenly. 'There are all those
relatives downstairs. You must go and tell them there
isn't going to be a wedding. However,' she added. 'The
first person you've got to see is Lorenzo. Not even he
deserves the sort of treatment and duplicity that he has
received from our family, and you've obviously got
some explaining to do. So, you'd better get on with it
while I try and find some aspirin. My head's killing me,
it really is.'

Coming back from the bathroom she found her sister
still sitting on the end of the bed, clearly wrapped up in
a happy day-dream. 'I thought you'd gone downstairs,'
she said in surprise. 'It's no good just sitting up here,
you've got to go down and face the music.'

'Oh no!' Claire stood up, yawning. 'I only got back
from America late last night, and I'm feeling absolutely
whacked . . . it must be the jet lag. So, I'm off to lie down
for a bit. Anyway,' she added with a laugh as she opened
the door, 'it isn't me that Lorenzo wants to see, is it?'

'Well, it certainly isn't me!' Darcy shouted angrily after Claire's departing figure. 'You ... you rotten coward ...'

Left alone, Darcy sat looking miserably at herself in the dressing table mirror. 'Oh Lord! What am I going to do?' she moaned, her spirits quailing at the magnitude of the task before her. Her father had, of course, only himself to blame for the mess he was now in, but ... but what about Lorenzo? How could she possibly bring herself to tell him about Claire?

She rose and began to slowly pace up and down, trying desperately to think of the right words, the right phrases to use in explanation of her father and sister's conduct. Lorenzo was clearly no fool and if there was not to be an almighty explosion, she would have to think up some convincing arguments.

But she couldn't, she realised with dismay. She simply wasn't able to think about anything other than Lorenzo's extraordinary behaviour. Her head throbbed angrily, her mind filled with an overwhelming feeling of personal outrage. How dared Lorenzo pretend that he and Claire had a ... a relationship which he knew very well that they hadn't? *How dared he!*

He must have assumed that buying the house and getting engaged had given him a sort of licence to behave in the way he had. All that business about Claire's passionate kisses, her tender embrace ...? Darcy ground her teeth in fury. She was absolutely sure that Claire was telling the truth and yet ... why should Lorenzo have told such whopping lies?

Darcy's face burned with shame as she remembered how she had responded to his practised lovemaking. Well, this wasn't Sicily, and if he thought such ... such conduct was acceptable, here in England, she would take the greatest pleasure in letting him know just how wrong he was!

Only she had to tell him she wasn't Claire, hadn't she? Darcy sighed with resignation. She was back, full circle, to the dreadful task which lay before her. If only she had more time to think, she shook her head distractedly, more time to go over, in her mind, the happenings of the week ... Maybe if she had some peace and quiet she could work out why Lorenzo had behaved so peculiarly, a question which at the moment her tired brain seemed completely unable to cope with.

With reluctant, hesitant steps she walked down the wide staircase, surprised to see through the half-landing window a stream of cars departing down the drive. She was even more puzzled to hear her father's angry voice coming from the sitting room as her mother jerked open the door and rushed towards the kitchen with tears streaming down her face.

Running swiftly into the room, Darcy looked in bewilderment at her father sitting huddled in a chair, his face in his hands and at her great-uncle Henry, who was standing by the window looking pink faced and indignant.

'What ... what's going on?' she demanded breathlessly.

'Ah—at last! Why don't you take off that ridiculous wig, Darcy?' a voice drawled softly behind her.

Without conscious thought she did as she was told, the long gold hair flying about her shoulders as she whirled to see Lorenzo leaning nonchalantly against the mantelpiece. Looking into his cool, dark eyes which gleamed with cynical amusement, she suddenly felt sick with fright.

'Y-you ... you know ...' she stuttered in confusion.

Lorenzo gave a sharp bark of sardonic laughter. 'My dear Darcy, I have always known that you were not who you pretended to be. That you were not ... er ... Claire.'

'But how? I don't ... I don't understand. I mean ...'

'Oh, for God's sake!' her father shouted angrily. 'That's the very least of our problems. And it's all the fault of this damn fool here!' He glared furiously at the bishop.

'I shall ignore and turn the other cheek to your blasphemy, Ralph,' the bishop intoned sanctimoniously.

'You won't have a cheek to turn in a moment, you half-wit!' the Colonel roared, jumping to his feet in fury.

'Father! For Heaven's sake—what's going on?' Darcy cried in bewilderment as the two elderly men glared angrily at each other.

Lorenzo gave a low laugh, moving forward, to pull her swiftly into his arms.

'What is "going on" *carissima*, is that your great-uncle Henry did not just go through the motions this morning,' he purred softly. 'The good bishop has just informed your parents, and myself, that you and I are indeed married—both in the sight of God and by law!'

CHAPTER FIVE

DARCY lay in the bath gazing at her luxurious surroundings with dull, uncaring eyes. It was more like a film set than a bathroom, she thought dispiritedly, sitting up and reaching for a flannel. Her movement in the round cream marble bath was immediately reflected in the shimmering floor-to-ceiling mirrors set between marble columns, which in turn reflected back the incandescent glow from the crystal lights and chandelier—who had ever heard of a chandelier in a bathroom?—and the smooth acres of deep cream carpeting. Even the ceiling was mirrored, she realised, flushing as she looked up and caught sight of her pale naked form floating in the vast bath that was surely designed for at least four people to bathe in comfort, not just one.

Lying back, she allowed the bitter, desperate tears of utter misery to flow freely down her cheeks for the first time since she had been told of her so-called 'marriage'. Darcy had been incapable of weeping as her numbed, shocked mind had struggled to assimilate Lorenzo's dreadful words. His harsh laugh had rung around the sitting room of Belmont Hall, his dark eyes staring intently down into hers had seared her mind, her very soul as the terrible import of his message had struck home.

'*Married?* I'm married . . . to . . . to you? I . . . *Oh no!*' Her strangled cry of disbelief had seemed to come from somewhere far away as she had slumped with shock in his arms. Only his firm embrace had prevented her trembling body from falling to the floor.

'No . . . no . . . absolutely not!' she had cried hysterically, tearing herself away from Lorenzo a moment later. 'If this . . . if this is your idea of some joke . . .?'

'Ah, *cara*. How could I make a joke about such a matter? The good bishop has pronounced that we are indeed man and wife—it is amusing, no?'

'Amusing!' Darcy's mouth kept opening and shutting like a fish, but there seemed no way she could possibly express her horrified reaction to the news.

Sinking down on to a sofa, she tried with every force at her command to try and bring her dazed mind to bear on Lorenzo's words. 'Father . . . there must be some mistake, surely? I mean, it was only a rehearsal, wasn't it? Father . . .? Answer me, for God's sake!' she cried.

Colonel Talbot shrugged unhappily. 'The old fool here tells me that it's all legal. You and Lorenzo signed the register, you see. It was all witnessed properly too,' he sighed heavily.

Darcy felt as if she was in the midst of a living nightmare. It couldn't be true. It couldn't be happening to her. This sort of thing just didn't happen to ordinary, normal people, did it? It was all too . . . 'Divorce,' she heard herself saying. 'If I'm really married, then we must have a divorce—that's all.'

'And exactly on what grounds, my dear wife, are you proposing to divorce me?' Lorenzo's rich, deep voice held a steely menace.

'Who cares?' Darcy cried wildly. 'There must be thousands of good reasons for a divorce, if I could only think of them. I mean . . . well, apart from anything else, you thought you were marrying Claire. That's mistaken identity, isn't it, Uncle Henry?'

The Bishop nodded thoughtfully. 'There you are! There you are, you see!' she babbled. 'That's just one of the grounds for an . . . an annulment. It's all right, Father. Lorenzo thought he was marrying Claire . . .'

'No, I did not.' Lorenzo's hard, firm voice punctured Darcy's bubbling, euphoric relief.

'Oh don't be silly—of course you did,' she waved her hand dismissively.

'Ah, *carissima*. I can see that all this has been a shock to you—yes? But surely you cannot have forgotten that I told you a few minutes ago that I knew all along that you were not Claire. Hmm?'

'W-what!' Darcy looked at his tall menacing figure with dazed eyes.

'Alas, pretty one. You were not ... er ... very successful. I knew from the first moment that you were not who you seemed.' His broad shoulders shook with suppressed laughter.

'I can't see what's so damned funny,' she snapped. 'How could you know?'

'Your nails,' he drawled simply.

'My what?'

'Your sister bites her nails, doesn't she? Now, *cara,* I am always prepared to believe in miracles, but that your sister should have suddenly grown her nails to the length of yours—that was an impossibility, was it not?' He raised a dark eyebrow in mocking cynicism.

'Oh Lord!' Darcy groaned miserably, remembering how he had stiffened on kissing her hands the first time she had met him, here in this room.

'But ... but ...' She tried to rally her shattered emotional forces. 'That could have been anyone—somebody else, I mean. You didn't ... you didn't know it was me, did you?'

'A few moments' reflection while I was changing for our ... er ... engagement party showed me that such a similarity must betoken a member of the Talbot family. A glance at the picture of you and your sister on the top landing, as I made my way downstairs that evening, made all very plain.

He laughed harshly. 'Oh yes, I knew straight away *who* you were, it only remained for me to find out *why* you should be taking part in such a masquerade. I can assure you that one does not have to be a genius to work that out, my darling wife.' Lorenzo's dark eyes flashed with contempt over her father's hunched figure.

'I'm not your darling wife,' Darcy shouted angrily, trembling as much for her father's folly in crossing Lorenzo as for her own predicament. Although her problem of course, was going to be easily resolved—in the courts if necessary. No one could force her to live with this detestable man, that much at least was certain.

'Oh yes, for the moment you are indeed my wife,' he answered with maddening imperturbability, a small smile playing on his sensual lips. 'Is that not so, my Lord Bishop?'

'What? Oh yes, yes . . .' Uncle Henry mumbled before drawing himself up to his full height. 'Those whom God hath joined together, let no man put asunder,' he boomed in a loud voice.

'Get that old fool out of here! Get rid of him, or by God I won't be responsible for my actions,' her father shouted angrily.

'Take not the name of the Lord in vain,' the Bishop murmured, carefully skirting the Colonel's trembling figure and moving swiftly towards the door. 'Bless you, my children,' he muttered in the direction of Darcy and Lorenzo as he made good his escape, almost colliding in the doorway with Mrs Talbot.

'Oh darling—I'm so sorry, I really am.' Darcy looked up with dazed blue eyes as her mother came to sit down beside her, holding her hands and looking sorrowfully into her face. 'Whatever you do, don't worry. I'll think of something.'

'I really don't think I can stand the thought of any more of your good ideas, Mother.' Darcy was ashamed to hear the wobbly note in her voice as she fought to control herself.

'No, well, I . . .' Mrs Talbot seemed lost for words and clearly terrified of looking in Lorenzo's direction. Getting out a handkerchief, she blew her nose loudly, giving her reddened eyes a surreptitious wipe.

'I do not wish to be awkward,' Lorenzo murmured, the note of irony quite evident in his mocking voice. 'However, I do wonder at the whereabouts of my . . . er . . . ex-fiancée?'

'Your ex-fiancée is upstairs,' Darcy told him bitterly. 'Why don't you go up and say hello? I'm sure she'll be delighted to see you, although I'm afraid she's just a little tired at the moment, having just flown back from America where she has apparently collected yet another fiancé!'

'Oh, my goodness,' her mother jumped up. 'I must go upstairs and see her straight away. I had no idea . . . Oh dear . . .'

'You won't get any change out of Claire, Mother. She's got a total fixation about her "darling Roddy" . . .' she called after her mother's disappearing figure.

'And . . . and as for you . . . you bloody man . . .!' she turned angrily on Lorenzo who was shaking with laughter. 'You can stop grinning like that right this minute! It's not funny . . . it's not funny at all.'

'Oh yes, my darling wife, it is!' His eyes gleamed boldly down at her flushed angry face.

'If you call me your "darling wife" just once more, I'll . . . I'll . . .' Darcy jumped up, almost choking with rage, her fists tightly clenched as she glared with hatred at the man she had supposedly married that morning.

'*Mannaggia!* That is enough,' Lorenzo growled ominously. His dark eyes held hers, glinting with menace as he moved towards her. 'You will now go to the library, where we can talk privately. We have much to talk over, have we not?'

'All I want is a d-divorce and . . . and n-never to have to s-see you again,' she wailed unhappily.

'We must therefore discuss our problem rationally and calmly. Come Darcy,' he said taking hold of her arm in a grip that brooked no denial.

She glanced fearfully up at the man towering over her, her mind refusing to function normally as he firmly and inexorably propelled her shaking figure towards the other room.

Darcy took a deep breath, turning around to face Lorenzo as he closed the library door and leaned casually against it. 'You must see, Lorenzo, that quite obviously a dreadful mistake has occurred. I . . . I can't defend my father's or my actions in the matter, but . . .'

'Sit down, Darcy,' he said firmly.

'There is no need for me to sit down. There's really nothing for us to discuss, now or in the future, except the details of a divorce. Surely all that can be left to our lawyers . . .?' She ran a distracted hand through her long hair.

'No. I think not.'

'I really can't stand much more of this nonsense, Lorenzo, so . . .'

'So, why do you not do as I ask and sit down. Hmm?'

Darcy hesitated, eyeing him warily. All her instincts warned her to cut this interview as short as possible. The hard dark eyes regarding her so coolly were disturbing, and she felt a spasm of fury against both him and her father for having placed her in such an invidious position.

Lorenzo sighed briefly as he eased his powerful body away from the door and walked forward to stand in front of her. 'I am telling you, for the last time, to sit down, *cara*,' he murmured softly.

'This is my house and I'll do what I . . . Oh!' she gasped as he calmly pushed her into the chair. 'How dare you!'

'How dare I?' he drawled silkily. 'Is it really necessary for me to remind you that it is not your house, Darcy? On the contrary, I understood that it was now mine. Correct me if I am wrong?'

She blinked nervously at the man who stood looking down at her with an unwavering gaze of ruthless implacability.

'I . . . yes, I . . .' She took a deep breath. 'Yes, of

course I realise that this house is now yours, Lorenzo, but . . .'

'There are no "buts" to be considered, Darcy . . . This is my house and you are my wife. I cannot really see, therefore, that we have anything to discuss.'

'Oh yes we damn well have!' she fumed, irritated afresh as she saw him lift one dark eyebrow in mockery at her defiance.

'Such as?' he murmured, moving to sit down opposite her trembling figure.

'For God's sake!' she gestured wearily. 'To start with, I don't want to be married to you.'

Darcy paused, her anger rising as he continued to regard her in silence from beneath his heavy eyelids. 'The very thought of being married to you fills me with . . . with repugnance,' she ground out through clenched teeth. 'Surely that's a good enough reason?'

'What a charming sentiment, my dear Darcy,' he purred with sardonic amusement. 'However, as matters stand, I do not feel that it is a sufficiently good reason to dissolve our marriage.'

'Well—that's just your bad luck!' she hissed, her face flushing with the effort of trying to control her frayed nerves.

'Yes, it would seem to be my bad luck, *cara*. Unless, of course, your father is proposing to pay me back the money I have given him for this house?' His voice was heavy with irony.

'Yes, I'm sure that . . .' She blushed a deep crimson as she realised that there was no way her father could ever repay all the money, even if he managed to get some of it back from the bank.

Lorenzo gave a low laugh. 'You are a bad liar, my Darcy, even if your loyalty to your family does you credit. However, since I am informed by my bankers that the second and last instalment was deposited in your father's bank two days ago; and that moreover he has no way of repaying me, it is an academic question, is it not?'

'Okay. So you've got the house. Fine! Great! But you don't need me as well!' She jumped to her feet and began to pace up and down the room in agitation.

'I made a bargain with your father, and I am expecting it to be honoured.' His voice hardened, the raw force of his personality becoming evident as he rose from his chair.

She whirled, the blood draining from her face. 'But that's crazy! You ... you can't want to marry me. I wouldn't suit you at all. In fact ... in fact it would serve you right if you did have to stay married to me. You'd hate it,' she assured him eagerly, desperately anxious that he should realise just how awful was the prospect of their marriage.

'But *cara*, I think that I have been "served right" as you put it. I see now that Claire would not have suited me at all, whereas you, my dear Darcy, you will do very well.'

'You're mad!' she gasped with horror. 'You're stark staring raving mad! Why should I suit you any better than Claire? And ... and anyway, if you knew all along that I wasn't my sister, you ... you were deceiving me. You ...'

'*I?*' he thundered, his face suddenly becoming the pitiless mask that she had always suspected lay beneath the lazy, amused smile he normally assumed. 'Are you suggesting that it is I who planned this whole despicable masquerade? Was it I who dressed up and pretended to be what I was not? *Well?*'

Darcy stared blindly at him, her eyes deep blue pools of acute misery. 'No ... I ... It was just to help my sister. I ...' She shook her head confusedly, as he came over to stand beside her, placing a hand beneath her chin and tilting her face up towards him. His unwavering scrutiny seemed to last for ever. A deep tide of crimson covered her face and she looked away, finding herself unable to meet his dark gaze.

'No, *cara*. It was you who thought you were fooling

me, no?' he purred with silky menace. 'But it did not quite work out like that, did it? However, I am content to have you as a wife. This is, after all the perfect house to bring up my children.'

'I ... er ... I didn't know that you had been married before,' she looked at him in bewilderment. 'How many children have you?'

'*Cristo!*' Lorenzo swore with impatience. 'For a clever woman—and I am reliably informed that you are a very clever woman, you are being particularly stupid today, Darcy. I have not been married before. I was referring to our children—yours and mine, of course.'

'*What!*' It took her some moments to assimilate the implication of his words, her body trembling with shock as their full import broke through the fog of her confused mind and registered firmly in her brain.

'You and I ...? Children ...?' she gasped in horror.

'They are the ... er ... natural outcome of marriage,' he drawled with evident amusement.

'You mean ... you mean that our marriage will ... that I'd be expected to ...' She couldn't continue, the frightening words seeming to stick in her throat.

'*Senz'altro*. Of course. We will have a normal marriage and you will indeed be expected to ... er ... share my bed,' he drawled smoothly.

'B-but I ...' Her stomach gave a painful lurch at the thought of his lovemaking, and her heart began to beat erratically. 'But I ... I don't even like you, in fact, I ... I hate you ...' she cried wildly, spinning on her heel and running towards the door.

She never reached it. With contemptuous ease, Lorenzo put out a hand and she found herself firmly trapped within his hard embrace. For a few timeless moments she stood imprisoned not only by his arms which tightened about her slim figure like bands of steel, but by his fierce piercing gaze which seemed to devour her very soul. As if in slow motion his dark head came down towards her, his mouth closing over hers in a kiss of ruthless possession.

She fought him as fiercely as she could, raining blows with clenched fists against his broad shoulders and any other part of his anatomy that she could reach. All in vain, as he adroitly captured first one wrist and then another, holding them in one of his large hands behind her back. His other hand slid sinuously over the delicate bones of her face and down the nape of her neck, holding her head firmly imprisoned beneath his mouth.

Exhausted and ceasing to struggle, she felt his lips become warm and tender, moving softly and sensuously over hers, evoking a response she couldn't control as a treacherous warmth invaded her trembling limbs. Moaning helplessly her lips parted under the delicate pressure, allowing him to savour the soft inner tissues of her mouth in a kiss of devastating invasion.

'Hate?' Lorenzo drawled with sardonic amusement as he withdrew his head and looked down at the dazed girl lying in his arms. 'No, I do not think that it is hate that you feel for me, *cara!*'

She could only stare blindly back at him, her eyes large shimmering pools of deep lapis lazuli in a face that had become increasingly pale and strained, as he outlined in every crude detail what he would do if she decided to terminate their marriage.

She might have been able to withstand Lorenzo's avowed intent to sue her father for the return of his money, Darcy thought as she stepped out of the deep marble bath, but she was helpless against his final threat.

Wrapping a thick white towel about her shivering body, she gritted her teeth to stop the tears from flowing again as she remembered his cruel words.

'I shall also, and very publicly, sue you for a dissolution of this marriage, outlining in every detail how an old English family sought to dupe a visitor to their country. I shall take particular pains,' he had added with a wolfish leer, 'to implicate your mother in this affair.'

She had gasped with horror at the disgrace and torture this would bring on the one member of her family for whom she cared very deeply, begging and pleading for mercy. Lorenzo had, however, remained obdurate, insisting that she give him her decision immediately.

If only, she moaned miserably to herself, if only she hadn't been feeling so shattered by everything that had happened that day. If only she had been given time to gather her scattered wits and have a period for calm reflection, for constructive thought. Instead of which, there had been no decision to make. She could not possibly let her poor mother endure the torment of his proposed court action, and slumping into a chair she had resigned herself to her fate.

From then on she had moved like an automatan through the day. Lorenzo, who had a business meeting in London late in the afternoon, insisted that they left Belmont Hall immediately. She hadn't even been given time to go upstairs and say goodbye to Claire, she remembered dully; nor to pack any clothes. She had nearly broken down at the sight of her mother's worried face as Lorenzo had given her the news.

'Are you sure, darling? Are you certain that this is what you want?' her mother had asked unhappily.

Under her new husband's eagle eye Darcy could only try to sketch a smile and try and reassure her mother that she was blissfully happy. Her words didn't convince either of them, of that she was certain. However, Lorenzo had given neither mother nor daughter time to discuss matters privately, hustling her out of the house with what she regarded as indecent haste.

The journey to London had been conducted virtually in silence as she had stared out of the window with dull, uncaring eyes, still not able to comprehend what was happening to her.

She had only spoken once. 'Why do you want Belmont Hall so badly, Lorenzo? And why me, when you know how much I . . . I loathe the thought of being married to you?' Her voice had rasped huskily as she turned her head slightly, glancing through her eyelashes at the aquiline, arrogant profile of the man beside her.

'Ah! I have very good reasons of my own for wanting your family home, Darcy. As for you . . .' he paused. 'Let us just say that I also have a good reason for wishing to possess you. *Perchè no?* You are a beautiful woman.'

'Hah!' Darcy had snorted with grim disbelief, lapsing back into a silent stupor as the sports car scorched its way down the motorway.

Not being a frequent visitor to London, she had no means of knowing exactly where she was as Lorenzo drove them through the crowded streets of the City, although she thought she caught a glimpse of the Bank of England before the car snaked around a corner and down into an underground car park.

He helped her out, tossing the car keys to a uniformed attendant, before issuing her before him to an iron gate which he unlocked with a key from the large bunch in his hand. Further gates were unlocked and locked again, even the lift needed a key to operate it, she noticed.

'What . . . I mean, where is this?' she asked with a nervous shiver as the iron gates clanged shut behind them.

'The Barbican. I find it very handy for my business in the City,' he replied briefly, as the lift sped upwards.

'Barbican—"a towered fortress". Very appropriate!' Darcy ground out through clenched teeth, her body trembling at the sight of the bare, stark walls.

'I think that you will find my . . . er . . . our apartment very comfortable,' he drawled smoothly as they arrived at the top floor.

'No,' she had said with an absolute certainty,

remembering the grim exterior of the vast complex. 'No, I feel as if I am in prison.'

If he heard her remark, Lorenzo chose to ignore it as he opened the front door of his apartment. 'Ah, Wilkins,' he said to the small man Darcy had seen at the engagement party. 'You have met Miss Talbot, have you not? You will be pleased to hear we were married this morning.'

Darcy awarded Lorenzo's manservant ten out of ten for only betraying by a small flicker of his eyes the undoubted shock of his master's news.

'May I offer my congratulations, sir, and to you, madam,' he smiled warmly at the tired looking girl.

'Come. You must meet Mrs Wilkins and then I think you should rest, no?' Lorenzo murmured, putting an arm about her waist and leading her towards what she assumed was the kitchen, but which looked more like the flight deck of a space ship.

Mrs Wilkins was a fat, jolly woman who beamed with pleasure at the news of the marriage.

'The Contessa is very tired. I wish her to sleep for some hours, and then you might wake her with some tea, Mrs Wilkins. At, shall we say, six o'clock?' He turned to lead Darcy's unresisting, numb figure to a suite of vast rooms.

'Your dressing room, my dressing room, the bedroom and the bathroom ...' Lorenzo moved around opening and closing doors, his words washing over her weary, exhausted figure as she stood in the middle of the bedroom, her feet sinking into the deep piled carpet as she stared about her with dazed eyes.

'You see, the view across London is very fine, is it not?' he said, going over to the wall of floor to ceiling windows and pushing a button. Fine, gossamer curtains closed across the view with a silky swish, blotting out the daylight as the room became dim and more intimate.

'It is not too prison-like, I hope *cara?*' he

murmured, coming to stand in front of the trembling girl and gently running a finger down her pale cheek. 'You must sleep now. You will feel better when you awake, yes?'

She had felt too miserable, a large constriction in her throat preventing her from saying anything as she shut her eyes to prevent the tears which filled her eyes from falling. *I won't give him the satisfaction of seeing me cry, I won't, I won't,* she told herself desperately, hearing the door click quietly behind his departing figure.

Stripping off her clothes, she crawled into the large bed, falling into an exhausted sleep as soon as her head touched the pillow.

Mrs Wilkins had, as instructed, woken her with a cup of tea on the dot of six o'clock. Presenting her also with a large box, which she said had just been delivered.

'Why don't you have a nice hot bath, madam? You'll feel ever so much better. Weddings can be very exhausting.'

'Yes, er . . . thank you, Mrs Wilkins. Darcy had smiled wanly up at the woman's kind face as she put on her horn-rimmed glasses. Waiting until she was alone, she undid the ribbon around the large box, pulling forth from the layers of tissue paper a froth of pale blue silk and lace, which separated out into a nightgown and negligee.

Darcy had gulped at the thought of wearing such an outfit, especially when she held up the nightgown against herself and realised with horror just how much it would display and emphasise the contours of her figure.

Wandering now back into the bedroom, the white towel wrapped tightly about her body, she looked with embarrassment at the garments laid out on the bed. I'll never be able to wear something like that, she thought, blushing with embarrassment. But, what else have I got to wear? Only what she had travelled in, she realised with a sinking heart.

Sitting down on the edge of the bed, she clasped her arms tightly about her body, trying to stop the nervous trembling which seemed to be shaking her slim form like a raging fever. She had to try and find a way out of this . . . this marriage. There must be a way through the maze, if only she could think of one, she told herself. A spasm of desperate longing for the calm, ordered peace of her Cambridge life seized her with such poignancy that it was all she could do not to burst into tears yet again.

So sunk in misery was she, that she was unaware of Lorenzo's arrival until she looked up to find him standing beside her, looking down at the dejected, hunched figure of his wife. 'You are not dressed, *cara*. Do you not like your negligee?' he murmured quietly.

'Yes, I'm sure it's . . . er . . . it's lovely, Lorenzo. It's just that I . . . er . . . I couldn't wear such a thing. Really I can't . . .' her voice trailed away unhappily, as he bent forward, taking her arms and raising her to her feet.

He laughed softly, looking down at his wife who was clutching the towel about her body with fingers that were white with tension, her fluttering eyelids and soft, trembling mouth indicating extreme nervousness.

'I am going to have a shower, *cara*. I suggest therefore that you go to your dressing room and change into your nightgown and negligee. We will be dining here tonight. Mrs Wilkins has left us a cold supper, and we will be quite alone, so there is no need to feel shy. Hmm?'

'I can't . . . I . . .'

'Ah, I see. You wish me to dress you, is that it?' he purred softly.

'*No!*' she gasped, and ran for her dressing room pursued by his sardonic laughter.

Darcy felt almost sick with apprehension as she looked at herself in the full length mirror. As she had suspected, not only did the nightgown reveal every bit of her figure as it sinuously rippled down over her body, but the effect of the negligee was even worse. Scooping low in front, it was designed to fasten under her bosom, throwing her full breasts in the thin nightgown into sharp relief. She blushed as she realised that there was no way of disguising the nipples which strained against the fine silk for all, and Lorenzo, to see.

A knock at the door broke into her reverie, and she jumped in fright as her husband entered the room wearing a thin silk, red dressing gown which clung to his broad shoulders and slim hips.

A deep tide of crimson spread over her face as he ran his eyes slowly over her figure. 'I . . . I can't wear this. It's . . . it's indecent . . .' she whispered, clasping her hands protectively over her breasts.

'On the contrary, you look charming,' he said moving towards her and gently taking her hands in his. 'Absolutely charming,' he repeated, huskily.

Darcy glanced quickly up at him, noting the absence of his usual sardonic tone, a fact that made her feel even more frightened if that were possible.

'Where . . . where did you get it?' she asked nervously as he led her through into the main room.

'Your negligee? I have no idea. I merely asked my secretary to arrange something suitable. She always has excellent taste.'

'You mean . . .' she looked at him aghast. 'You mean that she's bought this sort of thing before . . .?'

'Of course. I am thirty-six years of age, *cara*, and certainly not a monk!' He laughed at her horrified expression. 'Come, let us eat, yes?'

Darcy toyed with her food, unable to taste anything as she tried to fight the rising tide of panic that threatened to engulf her. She gulped down a glass of wine and indicated that she would like another. Maybe if she got drunk, it wouldn't be too bad . . .?

Lorenzo, with what she thought of as devilish clairvoyance, laughed as he poured her a second glass.

'That is all, my Darcy. I wish to have you awake and . . . er . . . fairly sober!'

'You're despicable!' she hissed, a sudden surge of anger taking over from her previous numbed acceptance of her fate. 'It's . . . it's rape—that's what it is!'

'Violenza carnale? Oh no,' he mocked heartlessly. 'I do not think it will be a matter of rape, my darling wife.'

'I may have the misfortune to be your wife, but I'm certainly not your "darling",' Darcy flashed him a look of pure venom as she quickly drank the second glass of wine.

If only someone would suddenly appear and rescue her. But who was there who even cared enough to . . . 'Oh no!' she cried, jumping up from her chair. 'I can't possibly stay here. I can't be married to you. I'm . . . I'm engaged to someone else . . . well, almost engaged . . . Oh no!' She buried her face in her hands as she thought longingly of Richard. He would never threaten her like this dreadful man. Richard had always been so kind and gentle, he . . .

'Sit down and calm down,' Lorenzo commanded. 'Richard Petrie would not have done for you at all. A nice man but far too milk and water for such as you.'

'How did you know about Richard?' she asked in astonishment, sinking back defeated into her chair.

'I know many things,' he smiled cynically at her pale face. 'I do not know, however, whether you have slept with him. It is . . . er . . . important,' he added gently as she blanched at his words.

'I . . . it's none of your damn business! I . . .'

'Darcy—do not attempt to play games with me.' His icy drawl sent shivers of fear down her spine. 'Ah no . . . I think not . . .' he mused softly as she blushed beneath his intense gaze.

'Of course I've had lovers,' she cried defiantly. 'Lots and lots . . .'

'You, my darling, have had lots and lots of wine on

an empty stomach,' he grinned, rising to sweep her protesting figure up into his arms in one fluid movement, before striding purposefully towards the bedroom.

'I hate you, I hate you!' she cried, struggling desperately as he approached the large bed.

'Ah, that is better,' he murmured, pinning her body to the bed as he slowly removed her glasses. 'That is how I saw you coming down the staircase at our engagement party. It took me some moments to work out why you should have had such an enchantingly wide-eyed and haughty look on your face.'

'Because . . . because I'm blind without my glasses—that's why!' she ground out through clenched teeth as she fought against the weight of his hard form.

'I know. I know everything about you, *carissima*.' His soft whisper was the last she heard as for what seemed an eternity she fought him, tossing her head from side to side as she tried to avoid the mouth that was stifling the screams in her throat. Her struggles growing weaker, he gently kissed away the helpless tears, soothing the body which quivered beneath him with warm caresses at once tender and dominating.

It wasn't until she lay utterly exhausted and quiescent in his arms, her slim frame racked by deep sobs, that he began to make love to her. With consummate skill and patience he slowly removed her negligee and nightgown, his mouth and hands erotic instruments as he gently coaxed her body to a finely tuned sensual pitch that knew nothing except a deep aching need for physical release.

She moaned helplessly as his lips and fingers seemed to scorch her trembling body. No one had ever touched her like this before, no one had been so completely the master of all her most inner secrets and desires. Feelings and sensations she could not have dreamed existed flashed into life as her flesh seemed to melt beneath his overwhelming control of her emotions.

Sinking beneath great waves of pulsating desire she was unaware of the increasing urgency of his own passion, the deep husky groan torn from his throat as she moved her body sensually and wantonly against him. From the depths of her abandonment she gave an almost silent scream at his first painful thrust, and then she was lost. Lost in the sweeping storm of his hungry possession as he lifted them both to a peak of mutual ecstasy.

CHAPTER SIX

'COME, eat up Darcy. We have much to do,' Lorenzo commanded as they sat having breakfast. 'I'm afraid that I can only give you one morning of my time. I wish it could be more, but alas I have many pressing business affairs to deal with.'

He paused and looked across the table at his wife who was staring fixedly down at her plate of scrambled eggs on toast. 'You do not seem to be hungry, *cara*. Surely after ... er ... after such exercise you should have a good appetite hmm?' he added with a low laugh.

Darcy sat in silence, the long curtain of her gold hair falling forward to mask most of her face from his view, but not enough she realised to hide the deep blush which suffused her features at his words. Ignore the swine! she told herself, desperately trying to banish the memories of last night and earlier this morning. But, oh dear God, how her head ached! Her whole body, in fact.

She lifted a shaking hand to her brow, resting her elbow on the table for support as she pushed aside her plate. Wearily she closed her eyes, hoping to somehow eradicate the hard, indomitable features of her husband which seemed to be etched permanently on her mind. Never, in her whole life, had she felt so defenceless, so ready to burst into tears as she did at this moment.

Unaware that Lorenzo had risen from the table, she turned with a sudden spasm of fear as his hand brushed back the long length of her hair, her cheeks burning as she felt the intense gaze from Lorenzo's glinting dark eyes. She gave an involuntary shiver as his fingers trailed slowly over the delicate bones of her face, his thumb gently tracing the outline of her soft, trembling lips.

'Come,' he said softly, helping her to rise from her chair. 'We have much to do and very little time to do it in.'

'Where ... where are we going?' she asked with a nervous shiver as they left the apartment and descended down into the underground car park of the large Barbican complex.

The Ferrari's powerful engine roared into life as he turned the ignition key. 'You are a potentially beautiful woman, Darcy. I am merely going to prove it to you. To act like ... er ... Pygmalion, if you like,' he added with a low laugh as the sports car boarded the ramp and entered the busy streets of the City.

'Well, I'm certainly no Galatea!' she snapped with a sudden spurt of anger.

'Ah ha! What a joy it is to possess an intellectual wife.' He turned his head to grin sardonically at her flushed cheeks. 'Nevertheless, I am going to breathe fresh life into you and you will then be indeed a raving beauty.'

'I have no desire to be a ... a raving beauty,' she muttered furiously. 'I just want to go back to Cambridge, and ...' She couldn't continue as she felt a lump of misery constrict her throat.

'Those days are over. Finished,' he replied firmly in a stern, hard voice. 'You are now my wife and will behave accordingly.'

'But ... but that's a medieval attitude! Nobody ... nobody lives like that nowadays, not here in England, anyway.'

Lorenzo shrugged. 'Although I had an English mother, I am nevertheless pure Sicilian in my attitude to my wife, Darcy. I do not wish there to be any misunderstandings between us on that point.'

'Oh, I've got the message, Lorenzo,' she ground out in fury. 'Your wife is expected to know her place, isn't she? And ... and as far as you are concerned that would s-seem to b-be the b-bedroom!' she stuttered, almost overwhelmed by her feelings of impotent rage against the powerful, commanding figure sitting so calmly beside her.

'You have put that a trifle ... er ... crudely, *angelo mio*,' he drawled, his voice heavy with ironic amusement. 'However, in essence, you are of course quite correct!'

'God! How I ... I hate and despise you!'

'Really? How extraordinary!' The silky ruthless tone in his voice caused her body to shiver with apprehension. 'I thought that I had demonstrated quite clearly to you last night and indeed again this morning, that whatever it is you feel for me it most definitely isn't "hate"— hmm?'

'It ... it certainly isn't love!' she spluttered in helpless rage as his soft low chuckle echoed around the small enclosed space of the sports car.

'Ah, who knows, *cara*. You may indeed come to love me—quite madly. *Perchè no?*' he drawled imperturbably.

'*Why not?*' Darcy knew that she was rapidly losing control as she felt her body shake with fury. 'You may think that you're God's gift to women, but as far as I'm concerned you're nothing but a ... a disgusting animal—that's why not!'

Lorenzo did not reply as he slid the car into a parking place and cut the engine. He turned in his seat, the silence lengthening between them as she stared fixedly out of the window.

'What a termagant you are, my darling wife!' he said at last. 'I can see that it may take me some time, but do not doubt that I will tame you in the end.'

The lazy amusement in his voice goaded her almost to distraction. '*Never!*' she cried wildly, her hand flying towards his face. It never reached its destination and she moaned in pain as his strong fingers caught and held her wrist in a merciless grip.

GIVE YOUR HEART TO HARLEQUIN®

FREE!

Mail this heart today!

AND WE'LL GIVE YOU
4 FREE BOOKS, A FREE TOTE BAG, AND A FREE MYSTERY GIFT!

❧ IT'S A ❧

HARLEQUIN HONEYMOON

A SWEETHEART

OF A FREE OFFER!

4 NEW "HARLEQUIN PRESENTS"–FREE! Take a "Harlequin Honeymoon" with four exciting romances—yours FREE from Harlequin Reader Service! Each of these hot-off-the-presses novels brings you all the passion and tenderness of today's greatest love stories…your free passports to bright new worlds of love and foreign adventure!

But wait…there's <u>even more</u> to this great <u>free offer</u>…

HARLEQUIN TOTE BAG–FREE! Carry away your favorite romances in your elegant canvas Tote Bag. At a spacious 13 square inches, there'll be lots of room for shopping, sewing and exercise gear, too! With a snap-top and double handles, your Tote Bag is valued at $6.99—but it's yours free with this offer!

SPECIAL EXTRAS–FREE! You'll get our free monthly newsletter, packed with news on your favorite writers, upcoming books, and more. Four times a year, you'll receive our members' magazine, Harlequin Romance Digest!

<u>Best of all,</u> you'll periodically receive our special-edition Harlequin Bestsellers," yours to preview for ten days without charge!

MONEY-SAVING HOME DELIVERY! Join Harlequin Reader Service and enjoy the <u>convenience</u> of previewing four new books every month, delivered right to your home. Each book is yours for only $1.75—<u>20¢ less per book</u> than what you pay in stores! Great savings plus total convenience add up to a sweetheart of a deal for <u>you</u>!

START YOUR HARLEQUIN HONEYMOON TODAY–
JUST COMPLETE, DETACH & MAIL YOUR FREE OFFER CARD!

HARLEQUIN READER SERVICE
⊶§ FREE OFFER CARD ₷⊶

PLACE HEART STICKER HERE

FREE TOTE BAG

FREE HOME DELIVERY

4 FREE BOOKS

PLUS AN EXTRA BONUS "MYSTERY GIFT"!

☐ YES! Please send me my four HARLEQUIN PRESENTS ® books, _free_, along with my free Tote Bag and Mystery Gift! Then send me four new HARLEQUIN PRESENTS books every month, as they come off the presses, and bill me at just $1.75 per book (20¢ less than retail), with no extra charges for shipping and handling. If I am not completely satisfied, I may return a shipment and cancel at any time. The free books, Tote Bag and Mystery Gift remain mine to keep!

108 CIP CAJM

FIRST NAME_____LAST NAME_____
(PLEASE PRINT)

ADDRESS_____APT._____

CITY_____

PROV./STATE_____POSTAL CODE/ZIP_____

PRINTED IN U.S.A.

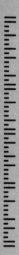

BUSINESS REPLY CARD

First Class   Permit No. 70   Tempe, AZ

Postage will be paid by addressee

Harlequin Reader Service®
2504 W. Southern Avenue
Tempe, Arizona 85282

NO POSTAGE
NECESSARY
IF MAILED
IN THE
UNITED STATES

Darcy quailed beneath the stern anger which swept across his tanned face, his sensual lips twisting into a ruthlessly cruel expression as he slowly removed her glasses. Still holding her wrist he jerked her sharply towards him, trapping her head between the edge of the wide headrest and his hard, firm mouth which descended to heartlessly crush her lips and punishingly force them apart.

Darcy found that she was totally immobile, completely unable to move and helpless beneath the force of his kiss. Tears filled her eyes as she moaned with defeat, her treacherous body responding to the tide of blood which seemed to race through her veins as he invaded the inner softness of her mouth.

'Ah, you are now quiet—that is better, no?' he murmured dryly, looking down into his wife's pale face as she gazed blindly back at him with bruised, deep blue eyes whose lashes were still spikey with tears.

Darcy lay back on her seat too dazed to move as he gently dried her eyes and replaced her spectacles before turning to open his door. He came around to help her out of the car, supporting her still trembling figure with his strong arm.

'Where ... where are we?' she asked bewildered, suddenly blushing as she realised that not only had he been kissing her in broad daylight, but in a public street in full view of the many passers-by.

'This is the back entrance to Harrods, the only place where I can obtain all I need for you in the short space of time that I have at my disposal.' He grasped her arm firmly and led her beneath the brown scalloped canopy over the door and into the hurly-burly of the large department store.

'I think ...' he paused. 'Yes, I think we will begin on the inside and work out.'

Darcy had absolutely no idea of what he was talking about as he dragged her swiftly towards the elevators. Minutes later she found herself in the lingerie department with Lorenzo calling for the manageress and imperiously stating his requirements. Pink with embarrassment, Darcy followed a salesgirl into a cubicle where, almost like a sleepwalker, she stepped in and out of the frothy confections of silk and lace which were brought for her to try on. Those that fitted were put on one side.

The salesgirl's eyes widened as the pile grew higher and higher. 'I don't know when you'll find the time to wear all those,' she giggled. Even Darcy was forced to smile, if a little grimly, at the enormous collection of bras, pants, cami-knickers (which she privately thought were rather rude), negligees and nightgowns.

At last it seemed as if Lorenzo had finished as the salesgirl returned empty handed. 'Your husband has asked that you should wear a new set of underwear since you are apparently going to try on clothes in the Designer Collection,' the girl informed her. 'Isn't he generous? You are lucky!' she sighed enviously.

If only you knew! Darcy thought sourly as she nevertheless complied with Lorenzo's demand. Walking beside him to the elevator she couldn't help relishing the feel of soft silk against her slim body.

'You see? Already you walk differently, more like a woman and less like a gawky schoolgirl,' Lorenzo murmured softly. 'Nice underclothes are very important for a woman.'

'And you know all there is to know about women, I suppose?' she hissed angrily, flashing him a glare of acute dislike.

'Yes,' he answered simply, his lips twisting in amusement as he watched her struggle to control herself as they were joined by other shoppers.

Well, he certainly seemed to know about women's clothes, Darcy thought, looking about her with glum resignation as Lorenzo and the manageress of the dress department discussed the various aspects of her figure, height and what they referred to as her 'true style'. 'I might as well be a tailor's dummy,' she muttered angrily as she was led away to a changing room.

Very soon Darcy lost touch with reality as she knew it. The dresses, suits and coats kept coming in a constant stream, all bearing such famous labels as Jean Muir, Daniel Hechter and Umberto Ginocchietti. When it came to evening wear, Lorenzo's choice was applauded by the manageress. By-passing such glorious, romantic dresses as those by Gina Fratini, he chose instead sinuous silk creations that skimmed and emphasised her slender body.

Hours seemed to pass as Darcy moved like an automaton, modelling each dress in turn until, as she stood swaying with fatigue, Lorenzo called a halt. Glancing at his watch he instructed her to hurry up and change back into some wine-coloured silk culottes and a matching silk blouse that he had particularly liked, while he arranged for all the clothes to be delivered tomorrow. 'All, that is, except for this,' he picked up a thin stream of fluid black silk. 'This we will take with us now.'

'Hurry up, *cara*,' he urged as they walked back towards the car. 'I must return you to the apartment for lunch before your appointment with the optician.'

'The . . . the what?' she queried, feeling so tired that she didn't know how she managed to put one foot in front of another.

'Those horn-rimmed glasses must go,' he informed her in a tone that brooked no argument. 'Great strides have been made in the field of contact lenses lately, and we must find you a pair that are comfortable, must we not?'

'Yes, Lorenzo—anything you say,' she sighed, lying back against the head-rest of the car and closing her eyes in exhaustion.

'So compliant—so submissive, Darcy? Unbelievable!' he murmured ironically as he drove swiftly through the streets. She found that she couldn't summon the strength to reply as waves of tiredness engulfed her weary brain.

Darcy gasped as she entered the large main room of the apartment. Everywhere she looked there were piles and piles of boxes. So many, in fact, that it took her some moments to realise that sitting amidst them was a small sandy-haired girl who was giving her a warm smile.

'Ah Jane. I can see that you have been busy!' Lorenzo laughed. 'You haven't met my new wife, have you?' he asked before turning to Darcy. '*Cara*, this is Jane Gordon, one of my right hands and your escort for the rest of the day.'

'Please accept my congratulations, Contessa,' Jane smiled at her, wrinkling her nose at the boxes which threatened to swamp the room. 'I'm sorry it's all such a mess, but I only had your shoe size to to on, and well . . .' she laughed. 'I decided to play safe!'

Darcy found herself smiling wanly back at the girl.

'I must return to my office and attend a working lunch. Wilkins will serve your meal when you are ready, *cara*, and I shall return at six o'clock.' Lorenzo stepped forward and took her weary figure in his arms. 'You look very lovely in your new clothes,' he breathed softly, brushing his mouth across her lips and smiling down with lazy amusement at her obvious embarrassment at being kissed in front of his assistant.

Left alone, Darcy stared at all the boxes and then looked helplessly at Jane Gordon. 'These . . . these are all shoes?'

'Shoes from Gucci and Rayne, handbags and scarves from Hermes,' the girl answered. 'These were the Conte's instructions, but obviously you won't like everything I've brought along, and those that you don't will be returned.'

'I . . . um . . . well, it's been quite a day, already. Do you . . . would you mind if I don't try them all on now?'

Darcy pushed a limp hand through her hair as Wilkins came in to announce that lunch was ready.

'My . . . er . . . my husband said something about my visiting an optician,' she murmured as they sat down to a meal of cold meat and salad.

'Yes, we've got quite an itinerary!' the girl laughed. 'First the optician and then a facial and make-up tuition at Elizabeth Arden, finishing with a hair-dressing session at Leonard. I hope that will be all right, Contessa?' she asked as Darcy pulled a wry face.

'Yes, I suppose so. It's just that I can see I'm going to need the constitution of an ox if I'm to survive this life,' she answered gloomily. 'By the way, please . . . er . . . please could you call me Darcy? All this "Contessa" business, it's . . . well, until yesterday I was studying for my PhD at Cambridge, and it all takes a bit of getting used to, if you know what I mean?' she pleaded with a helpless shrug.

'Sure—why not, Darcy? Just as long as you call me Jane in return. It's been a whirlwind romance, I gather?'

'Well . . . er . . . yes,' Darcy replied in confusion as she handed Jane the salad bowl. 'I take it that you work for my husband,' she added quickly, anxious to change the subject into a safer channel. 'I know that it must sound a little odd, but what does he do? His occupation, I mean.'

Jane looked at her in startled amazement for a moment and then laughed. 'Wow! It must have been some whirlwind! You really don't know anything about Conte Montreale's business—nothing at all?' she asked incredulously.

Darcy sighed and stared down at her plate. 'It would be foolish for me to pretend that I know anything about the business world,' she said slowly. 'I've spent the last four years in and around Cambridge University—hardly the hub of the London Money Market, as I'm sure you'd agree!' She looked up, smiling ruefully at the girl in front of her.

'Fair enough,' Jane replied. 'I studied economics at Oxford and I know just what you mean. Well, basically, your husband started with a tanker fleet, which he inherited from his father who died when Conte Montreale was very young. This fleet he expanded and sold off—at the top of the market, of course!' she grinned. 'His profits from that deal were invested in the newly emerging petro-chemical industry which has since blossomed in Sicily, and from there his business has now become world wide.' Jane paused to collect her thoughts.

'There's a very good article in Time Magazine about the Conte's rise to . . . er . . . fame and fortune which I'll send you. I'm only one of his personal assistants,' she explained. 'He has four "aides" as he calls them—two men and two women—who deal with his day to day business. Exactly what investments he controls is really outside my province. However, at the moment I am personally very involved with your husband in a take-over battle for British Incorporated Chemicals.'

'But . . . BIC's a . . . a huge multi-national firm, isn't it?' Darcy looked at her with stunned eyes.

'Yes, but very badly managed. They've made some rotten investment decisions in the past which are now coming home to roost. As you can imagine, it's all a bit fraught in the office at the moment, which . . .' she paused, and then grinned. 'Which is why I was so surprised to find that the Conte had managed to find enough time to get married!'

'Yes . . . I . . . it was all a bit sudden . . .' Darcy groaned inwardly. What could she possibly say to this very friendly but obviously very clever girl that would in any way explain what had happened? She couldn't of course—it was all too unbelievable.

The sandy-haired girl laughed again, sheepishly grinning at Darcy. 'I'm sorry—I sounded very rude and I can assure you that I didn't mean to. I'm delighted for you both and so pleased for Conte Montreale. It's time he settled down and I think . . .' she put her head on one side regarding Darcy quizzically. 'Yes, I really think you're just the person to tame him.'

'*You're joking!*' Darcy laughed harshly before she remembered she was supposed to be a happy, blushing bride. And then she did indeed blush as she suddenly realised that this must be the girl who had bought the nightgown and negligee yesterday, and that it hadn't been the first time she had performed such a service for her employer.

'No, I'm not joking,' Jane replied, looking at the lovely girl whose heavy curtain of rich gold hair couldn't hide her flushed cheeks. 'And if you're thinking about all his other women—don't. Goo-goo eyes and a large bust are no match for an intelligent woman—as I'm sure you've found out!' She glanced at her watch. 'Heavens! We're going to be late for your eye man. We must rush.'

All I've 'found out' is that my new husband is a womaniser and a business tycoon—all of which I had more or less surmised before, Darcy told herself as she led the way down to the subterranean car park. So why she should be feeling so unaccountably depressed she had absolutely no idea.

Returning to the apartment four hours later, Wilkins informed her that the Conte had been delayed on business, but that he would be returning later to take her out to dinner. 'If that's all, madam,' he added, 'Mrs Wilkins and I will leave you now.'

'Yes, thank you, Wilkins,' she murmured, wandering into the large sitting room and going over to stare out at the rooftops of London.

She had never spent such an exhausting day in all her life, Darcy told herself, resting her weary head against the cool plate-glass window. The magnificent view blurred before her eyes as she feverishly tried to concentrate on something . . . anything . . . anything but the recollections of last night and this morning. 'I won't think about it—I won't!' she muttered, desperately striving to banish the insidious memories which insisted on flooding back into her tired brain.

She had been woken at first light by a feather-light touch that had teased and tantalised her languorous body. Opening her eyes she had gazed sleepily up at Lorenzo who was regarding her with an enigmatically watchful expression from beneath his heavy eyelids.

'*Buongiorno, cara,*' he had drawled silkily, his hands continuing to gently caress her soft skin.

For a moment she had looked back at him with dazed eyes before blushing a deep crimson as she recollected exactly why she was in bed with this . . . this man. Wriggling as far away from him as possible, she clutched the sheet to her body with trembling fingers.

'Is it late? It m-must be time for b-breakfast,' she stuttered nervously, flinching as he gave a low laugh and whipped away the sheet.

'I may be hungry, *mia sposa,* but not for breakfast!' he murmured, his eyes devouring her slim naked form. Almost paralysed with fright she watched as he reached forward and then too late—far too late—she tried to scramble off the bed. Her frenzied struggles were unavailing as with consummate ease he caught hold of her arm, pulling her writhing body towards his hard, muscular frame.

'Let me go . . .!' she spluttered in helpless rage, drumming her fists against his broad shoulders, infuriated by his low, throaty chuckle of lazy amusement as he ignored her puny blows with a carelessness that was galling.

'I hate you—I hate you!' she sobbed as his dark head came inexorably down towards her. The mouth possessing hers was warm and surprisingly gentle as he softly teased and slowly parted her trembling lips. She gasped as a flame seemed to ignite the blood in her veins, flaring through her whole being as his kiss deepened. A kiss that demanded her total surrender.

Her heart began to thump painfully, her body mindless to all else except an overwhelming need of fulfilment as he slowly lifted his head and looked down at the passionate desire glowing in her deep blue eyes.

'Is this how you hate, *carissima?*' he whispered with a slow, sensual smile before he lowered his head once more, his mouth seeking the wildly beating pulse at the base of her throat.

Darcy shivered uncontrollably at the tremors of delight that shivered across her skin, a shaft of exquisite pain exploding deep in her stomach as he trailed his mouth downwards, his lips finding and caressing the rosy tips of her breasts.

'*Affascinante* ... so lovely,' he murmured thickly, his mouth and hands caressing her warm, firm body, evoking helpless moans of submission as she responded instinctively and wantonly to his experienced touch.

His low husky laugh of triumph as she frantically reached up to draw him down to her was almost the last sound she heard. She was only aware of the blood pounding loudly in her ears, the aroused musky scent of his body and her blindly passionate response as he gently parted her legs, leading her with tender and infinite mastery to the peak of sexual fulfilment.

Darcy sighed heavily as she gazed out at the panoramic view of London. God knows she hated Lorenzo with a deep, burning resentment, but even more she hated her weak, treacherous body for its abject, slavish capitulation to his demanding possession.

The shrill ringing tones of the telephone interrupted her thoughts. Looking around, she eventually found the instrument on a desk by the window.

''Allo ...? Lorenzo darling ...?' A husky breathless female voice breathed down the line.

'No ... I ... er ... I'm afraid he's not here. I ...'

'You are the secretary, no? You please tell 'eem that Marissa, she miss 'eem so much. You give 'eem much

love and many, many kisses, yes? And tell 'eem to come
to Roma very soon. *Caio*.' The line went dead.

Darcy grimaced as she hunted through the drawers of
the desk for a pen and some paper to leave the message
for Lorenzo. Her fingers fumbled with a buff-coloured
file, allowing some photographs to slip out. Picking up
the file, she bent to gather up the contents and then
froze in astonishment.

Slowly, one by one, she looked at the large glossy
prints. They showed a tall girl laughing into the sun;
cycling along a river bank with her long hair blowing in
the wind; wearing cap and gown as she stood outside
the Senate House after her graduation ceremony—and
many more . . . *They were all of her!* What on earth was
Lorenzo doing with such a collection, when they had
only met a week ago? She peered down at the pictures
which seemed to have been taken over a considerable
period of time.

The phone rang again and she answered it
absent-mindedly, telling yet another woman that
Lorenzo wasn't available. Slowly replacing the receiver, she sat in numbed shock as she tried to
assimilate the fact that the photographs were a
complete record of the years she had spent at
university.

Why? Why, or indeed how, had Lorenzo had them
taken? For what purpose? She'd never even heard of the
man before he had become engaged to her sister . . .

With stiff fingers she carefully replaced the pictures in
the file and put it back in the drawer as she wearily
tried to grapple with the puzzle. She still hadn't been
able to solve it an hour and four more telephone calls
later.

'He must run a damn call girl service!' she shouted
aloud as she angrily replaced the receiver. The last
caller, someone called Susie, had been almost abusive.
'Who in the hell are you, *sweetie?*' she had demanded.
Darcy had relieved her exacerbated feelings and taken

considerable satisfaction in replying, 'Oh, no one important. I'm just his wife, *sweetie!*'

However, she realised that giving Susie—whoever she was—a rude shock was hardly the answer to the questions which kept pounding through her brain. Why had Lorenzo wanted Belmont Hall when he was living here in the lap of luxury? Why, having bought the house, had he honoured the crazy bargain he had made with her father? Why, above all, did he insist on maintaining the farce of their marriage? And now the photographs . . .?

It was suddenly all too much for her tired mind to cope with. Maybe a long, hot bath followed by a period of calm reflection might help her to see matters in a clearer perspective?

Half an hour later Darcy dried herself, slipped on her glasses and wrapped in a fresh towel walked slowly back into the bedroom, deep in thought.

'I can see that I will be accused of being a cradle snatcher!' Darcy jumped with fright as the rich, deep voice broke through the miasma of her thoughts. Turning, she saw that Lorenzo was lounging in the doorway of the bedroom, a tumbler of whisky in his hand.

'You look barely sixteen, wrapped in that towel,' he explained, his dark eyes sweeping over her figure which trembled nervously under his scrutiny.

'I imagine you have had a busy day, yes? I very much approve of your hairstyle, *cara*. Very much indeed.' He smiled warmly as he viewed the smooth head of golden hair drawn back into a loose knot at the nape of her neck. Moving over to a bedside table, he put down his glass and shrugged his powerful shoulders out of his suit jacket.

Darcy felt suddenly weak at the force of his smile, which seemed to be affecting her breathing in an alarming manner. 'I . . . I think I'll just get dressed . . .' she mumbled, retiring into her dressing room.

However, it seemed as if there was no escape as drink in hand, he slowly strolled into the room after her hurrying figure and seated himself in a comfortable armchair.

Was she to have no peace from this man? Darcy clutched her towel tightly as the feelings of anger and rage, which she had been forced to repress all day, suddenly became more than she could control.

'Busy?' she snapped. 'Oh yes, I've been busy, and not just at the opticians, the stupid make-up place and the hairdresser,' she scowled. 'Your damn phone has been going non-stop! There's a list on your desk of the six women who phoned—from darling Marissa who wants me to give you "much love and kisses", down to dear Susie who was not at all pleased to hear that you are married. I suggest,' she added in a withering tone, 'that you organise an answering service to see to your ... your love life!'

If she had hoped to annoy Lorenzo, she was doomed to disappointment. Darcy watched with mounting fury as he threw back his dark head and roared with laughter.

'Oh, *cara*, I have it in me to feel sorry for poor Susie who obviously received the rough side of your tongue! But surely,' he added softly, 'it cannot be that you are jealous—hmm?'

Smarting at the lazy amusement in his voice, she shrugged her shoulders nonchalantly. 'Why should I be jealous? It's nothing to me what you do with ... with other women.'

'Is it not?' he asked mockingly raising a cynical eyebrow. 'Nevertheless, it was ... er ... unfortunate and I will see that it does not happen again.' He continued to sip his drink, looking reflectively at the angry girl.

'I am now a married man,' Lorenzo said at last, his dark gleaming eyes boring into hers. 'Whatever my ... er ... activities before our wedding, I can assure you that I intend to take the vows I made to you very seriously—very seriously indeed.' His hard voice softened. 'You will have no reason to complain about my behaviour in the future, Darcy. I can promise you that.'

'That wedding was a complete charade, and well you know it!' she snapped. 'What you do or do not do is a matter of supreme indifference to me. And now, if you don't mind, I'd like to get dressed.'

'Of course I don't mind.'

'W-what . . .?'

Lorenzo gave a dry bark of laughter. 'My darling, I would be a strange husband indeed, would I not, if I minded watching you get dressed?'

Her eyes widened incredulously as he sat comfortably back in the armchair, sipping his drink, a sardonic smile playing about his sensual lips.

'I can't . . . I mean . . . You're nothing but a . . . a voyeur!' she cried angrily, shooting him a baleful glare that would have felled a lesser man.

'A voyeur? Oh no, *cara*. I do not think so,' he purred silkily. 'Surely a voyeur is someone who watches women secretly, whereas I merely wish to view the sight of my wife dressing. A very normal, healthy desire I can assure you!'

Darcy found herself trembling with rage as his low laugh rang around the room. 'It's . . . it's disgusting! No decent . . . no decent Englishman would think of such a thing!'

Lorenzo's hooded eyes glinted with mockery as he shook his head sorrowfully. 'But alas, my darling. I am Sicilian. I do not, therefore, understand such nicities of behaviour. You must give up all hope of any civilised conduct as far as I am concerned. *Ha capito?*'

'Oh, I . . . I *capito* very well, you . . . you bastard!' she cried wildly, looking about her desperately for some avenue of escape.

In one fluid motion Lorenzo rose from the chair,

striding lithely towards her trembling body. Darcy backed nervously away, coming to rest against the mirrored cupboard doors as she looked fearfully up at the tall figure looming over her.

'Ah, you Englishwomen,' he murmured softly, removing the pins from the knot at her neck and shaking free the fragrant cloud of gold hair. 'So very, very cold on the surface. So frozen! Such ice!'

'Oh no—please! It took ages to do my hair ...' She shivered uncontrollably as his hand slid slowly down her neck, his fingers slightly brushing the full swell of her breasts revealed by the towel, which seemed to be slipping from between her shaking hands.

'Ah, but underneath ...? Ah, that is different, is it not, *carissima*?' he whispered, his mouth trailing across her cheek towards her trembling lips with deliberately arousing languour. 'Underneath there is such fire, much passion, no?'

'No ...!' she moaned, her large blue eyes widening in despair as she glimpsed the glittering desire from beneath his heavy eyelids. 'Let me go, Lorenzo ...'

Her husky plea was ignored, obliterated by the pressure of his mouth. A pressure that ruthlessly demanded her total surrender to his possession as one strong arm closed about her waist while with his other hand he removed the towel.

Gradually his mouth softened, his lips evoking a response she was unable to resist. His hands moved caressingly over her soft skin, igniting her senses and causing her to moan huskily deep in her throat at his sensual, erotic touch. Helplessly in the thrall of passionate desire, she clutched at him for support, frantically burying her fingers in his hair as her body quivered in his arms.

A moment later he lifted his head, gently unwinding her arms from his neck as she gazed at him, her large blue eyes cloudy with overwhelming desire.

'Continue to hate me like that, Darcy,' he said

thickly, 'and I will have no cause for complaint. However we will be late for dinner if we do not hurry, so I will leave you to get dressed—alone!' He laughed gently as he strode across the room, closing the door behind him.

Darcy leant weakly against the cupboard, trying to collect herself as her body throbbed and ached for sexual satisfaction, every nerve crying out for relief. Feeling almost sick with shame, she struggled into the thin wisp of silk suspenders, doing up the silk stockings with shaking fingers. 'You will never wear tights again, *cara*,' had been another of Lorenzo's imperial pronouncements she remembered, her brain almost bursting with loathing of the man who now so dominated her life.

She had just finished dressing when Lorenzo re-entered the room. Darcy could feel her knees tremble at the sight of his tall, immaculately dressed figure as his eyes travelled slowly over her shimmering black silk dress.

Expertly cut, the rich material clung caressingly to her body, outlining the curve of her full breasts, her slim waist and slender hips.

'Now, that is how I like to see you,' he said, moving forwards and turning her to face the floor-length mirror as he fastened a wide pearl choker with a large sapphire and diamond clasp in front, around her neck. Darcy's lips parted in a soft gasp, both at the magnificence of the gift and the feel of his fingers as he gently brushed them over the hard tips of her breasts which were to be clearly seen thrusting againt the silk bodice of her dress.

'You see?' he murmured, and looking at herself, she did indeed see what he meant, blushing a deep crimson and turning her tortured eyes away from a sight which made her writhe inwardly with shame.

'That, my darling,' he added softly, 'is a picture of a woman who is aflame for the touch of her lover. And that is how as your lover—and your husband—I shall enjoy looking at you tonight.'

'You ... you monster!' she moaned, fighting to control the weak tears which threatened to flow at any minute.

'Ah, *carissima*. How can I be such a monster, when I am simply anticipating the honey-sweetness of your body? Merely contemplating with pleasure the thought of you quivering in my arms as you tell me how much you want me—hmm?'

'Never!' she gasped. 'I'll ... I'll never do that.'

'Will you not?' He gave a low, mocking laugh, running a tanned finger down her flushed cheek before leading her trembling figure from the room.

'I thought we would dine by ourselves tonight, Darcy,' Lorenzo said as he issued her into the warmth and noise of Langan's Brasserie. 'There will be plenty of time for you to meet my friends later.'

Still shaken by her raw, lacerated emotions, she watched with nervous misery the constant stream of women, most of them quite ravishingly beautiful, who flocked to their table and greeted Lorenzo with enthusiastic fervour. If these are a sample of his 'friends' I think I'd prefer his enemies, she thought with glum resignation as a dark girl with flashing eyes and a truly amazing bust threw her arms about his neck.

It wasn't until she had almost finished her hors-d'œuvre that it occurred to her that for someone who was supposed to be a womaniser, Lorenzo was behaving slightly out of character. As each new arrival approached their table, he introduced Darcy as his new wife, talked to them for a moment or two and then politely but firmly sent them away.

Most of the women smiled wryly, casting puzzled looks at Lorenzo's silent and bespectacled wife as they accepted their dismissal with friendly resignation. Darcy could only helplessly agree with their unspoken thoughts summed up by one lovely girl's muttered observation, '... not his usual type, is she?'

No, I'm certainly not, she told herself, a heavy lump

of depression settling in her stomach at the thought of the other women's beauty and sophistication.

Half way through their meal, Darcy glanced up to see a dramatically beautiful girl with flaming red hair, bearing down on their table.

'Ah, Susie,' Lorenzo murmured. 'I believe you have already met my wife on the . . . er . . . telephone.'

Darcy winced at the sardonic amusement in his voice which the girl quite clearly didn't catch, being far too concerned with her own angry thoughts.

'I still can't believe it, Lorenzo darling! You can't have been mad enough to marry her . . .?' she gestured in helpless amazement, her green eyes flashing with venomous contempt at Darcy, before she turned to smile seductively at Lorenzo. 'You must be out of your mind, darling!'

Darcy stared fixedly down at her plate as Susie's harsh, incredulous laugh rang around the restaurant. She could feel her cheeks burning with shame and embarrassment as she imagined the other diners' amusement at the scene being conducted before them.

There was silence for a moment as Lorenzo beckoned to a waiter. 'Would you be good enough to conduct this lady to a table on the other side of the room?' he commanded in a voice soft with menace. 'My wife and I came here for a quiet meal and we do not expect to be interrupted in this fashion.'

'For Heaven's sake, darling! There's no need to be so stuffy . . .' Susie protested in a high, thin voice.

'Is there not? I suggest that you dine elsewhere since I find you ineffably boring and definitely *de trop*,' Lorenzo said dismissively as he took up his knife and fork to resume his meal.

Darcy waited with trembling apprehension for the storm to break about their heads. Instead of which she was astounded to see Susie's face pale and crumble into unhappiness, her drooping figure turning to accompany the waiter with laggard steps.

'You ... you were very unkind to that poor girl,' Darcy murmured, stealing a fearful glance at Lorenzo's harsh, autocratic features.

'Was I?' he queried blandly with a shrug of his powerful shoulders. 'It is a matter of no importance. Would you like some more wine, Darcy?'

She could only shake her head, completely unable to speak as she realised just how frighteningly hard and cruel her new husband could be. I'll never be able to stand up to him, she told herself in helpless misery. Absolutely never. Where on earth was she to find the courage to oppose such a forceful and ruthless personality?

Darcy knew it had been spineless of her to have so weakly agreed to accompany Lorenzo to London after the farce of their wedding, but what else could she have done? There was no one she could rely on, no one to whom she could turn for help. She was firmly and inexorably trapped in a tangled web from which there seemed no possibility of escape.

CHAPTER SEVEN

'I'M sick and tired of being ordered here, there and everywhere!' Darcy glared angrily at Lorenzo as they stood beside his private jet on the tarmac runway of Heathrow Airport.

Given no more than two hours' notice of their departure to Sicily, she had protested in vain that she couldn't possibly pack in time, that she wanted to say goodbye to her mother and Claire and that, above all, it was extremely unreasonable of Lorenzo to insist on her wearing a short, white lace dress whose high round neck and long sleeves meant that it was hot and scratchily uncomfortable to wear.

'Not to mention the fact that white is a totally unsuitable colour for travel,' she added in withering tones.

'It is precisely because I did not wish to endure days of futile arguments that I arranged our departure in such a way,' he retorted with an infuriating grin. 'Climb up into the aircraft, *cara*, or I will carry you up the steps myself.'

Despite his smile, the steely menace in his voice left her in no doubt that he would carry out his threat. 'Oh—all right, all right . . .' she muttered glumly as she obeyed his command.

The luxurious comfort of the wide leather armchairs was very different from the aeroplane seats in which she had travelled in the past, and by the time they were airborne and the young stewardess had served her with a long, cool drink, Darcy began to simmer down.

With a sigh she looked out of the window at the floating clouds. It was a complete waste of time arguing with her husband, she reminded herself bitterly. From the very start of her ghastly marriage he had totally dominated her life.

During the past fortnight her days had been filled to overflowing with visits to the hairdresser, the manicurist, and endless fittings at some of the top couturiers for yet more clothes—as if she didn't already have far more than she could possibly ever wear! On top of which, she thought grimly, she must now be one of the healthiest women in London if the daily strenuous exercise and massage sessions at an exclusive health club were anything to go by.

Every waking minute seemed to have been spent chasing from one part of London to another in a frantic attempt to keep up with the various appointments arranged by Lorenzo. Lorenzo who, despite running a large company engaged in a mammoth take-over battle, had still managed to find the time to ruthlessly organise every hour of her day.

Showered with jewels, surrounded by all the luxury that money could buy, Darcy realised that she ought to be more appreciative of what most people would regard as her good fortune. She was well aware that what she thought of as a prison-like existence was a way of life for which most women would sigh with envy.

In one of her few free moments she had read the article in Time Magazine which, as promised, Jane Gordon had sent over to the apartment. Headlined *Lorenzo the Magnificent*, it had fleshed out the bare bones of her new husband's dramatic rise to financial prominence and fame. Darcy had found no difficulty in reading between the lines the reporter's firm conviction that Lorenzo was a twentieth-century pirate who had in the past sailed perilously close to the rocks of financial insolvency, taking chances that would have surely bankrupted a lesser man.

Now of course, as the journalist had been at pains to point out, Lorenzo di Tancredi's affairs were as solidly based as the Bank of England and he was confidently expected to complete his successful takeover of British Incorporated Chemicals.

The article had been liberally illustrated with photographs of Lorenzo with his arm about one internationally famous and beautiful woman after another. Darcy was completely unable to understand why a man, whose lovelife was obviously so extensive, should have so meekly accepted the appalling *fait accompli* of his marriage to a girl he didn't even know.

The morning after she had found them, she had gone to look again at the file of photographs in the desk—only to find that they had disappeared. Maybe they had been a figment of her imagination, Darcy had thought, grinding her teeth in frustration as she sat one morning at the hairdresser's, desperately trying to find an answer to her difficulties. It's all Claire's fault, she had mused unhappily. If it hadn't been for Claire's engagement to Lorenzo . . .

'That's it!' Darcy suddenly laughed aloud, causing the assistant who was brushing out her hair to beam with pleasure at what he obviously thought was a compliment to his handiwork.

That was definitely it! There was no doubt in her mind that Claire must hold the key to the dreadful predicament in which Darcy found herself. That sister of mine has a good deal of explaining to do, she told herself grimly, realising with a sudden jolt that she hadn't been able to have a talk with Claire since the dreadful scene in the sitting room at Belmont Hall, when Lorenzo had informed her of their marriage. Whenever Darcy telephoned her old home it was always her mother who answered, breathlessly preoccupied with the trauma of trying to pack up and leave a house that had held the same family for almost five hundred years. So how was she going to manage to get hold of Claire and have a long, serious talk?

Having made her plans, she waited the next morning with mounting impatience for Lorenzo to leave for his office and then, feeling ridiculously guilty, she slipped out of the apartment. With her driving licence firmly clutched in her hand, she had hired a small car for the day.

Darcy knew that Lorenzo would be furious when he found out, but she simply didn't care, she told herself, almost intoxicated with her sudden freedom as she drove away from London, back to her old home in Suffolk.

She found her mother and Claire sitting in the kitchen surrounded by stacks of china and taking a well-earned rest from their labours. So delighted had she been at the thought of seeing them both again, that she was startled and disconcerted at their initial reaction to her arrival.

'I'd never have believed it—absolutely never!' her mother gasped, gazing wide-eyed at her eldest daughter. From the shining head of smooth golden hair caught into a loose knot at the base of Darcy's neck, her eyes travelled down over the dark blue, deceptively simple, silk dress, blinking slightly at the large sapphire and diamond brooch before noting the pure silk stockings and high-heeled navy court shoes.

'It's either a miracle or a mirage!' Mrs Talbot shook her head in wonder. 'When I think how you used to tie your hair back with those dreadful rubber bands, not to mention the skirts and jumpers from the Oxfam shop ... Well!'

'Good Lord! Talk about a caterpillar becoming a butterfly ...!' Claire echoed her mother's sentiments, looking with amazement at her sister's transformation.

'Oh come on! What's wrong with you both—I'm still the same person,' Darcy protested uneasily as Claire reached forward and took her hand.

'What a yummy watch! Are those really diamonds?' she asked, gazing at Darcy's wrist in awe. 'And where are those ghastly horn-rimmed glasses?'

'Well, I ... er ... I wear contact lenses now, they're

... er ... very comfortable,' Darcy muttered, disregarding her sister's first question as her face reddened with embarrassment. She felt such a fool standing here in the comfortable old kitchen, dressed up to the nines like this. She had become so used to complying with Lorenzo's insistence that she should be beautifully groomed at all times, and so preoccupied with her escape this morning, that she hadn't given a thought to the effect her appearance would have on her mother and sister.

'Anyway,' she added brightly. 'I'm not here to discuss me. I want to hear how the move's getting on.'

'Isn't it wonderful, darling,' her mother enthused, pouring Darcy a cup of coffee. 'Dear Lorenzo has told us that he will buy all the paintings and most of the larger pieces of furniture—anything we don't want, in fact. Your father is so happy to be keeping it all in the family.'

'I bet he is,' Darcy replied with a wry shrug at the thought of her father achieving his heart's desire.

'... and the marvellous thing is,' Mrs Talbot continued in full spate, 'the extra money will mean that we can afford a little house which Lorenzo has found for us around the corner from your father's club in London. Lorenzo has said that he will handle the purchase for us—isn't he kind? He made it all sound so easy when he flew up yesterday and ...'

'He did what?' Darcy gasped in surprise.

'Oh my dear,' her mother smiled. 'I suppose I will get used to that dreadful helicopter of his eventually, but as he says, it's so much quicker than travelling by car.'

'As far as I am concerned,' Claire chimed in with a laugh, 'the really good news is that your dear husband has booked the removal vans and they, thank God, are going to pack all the china for us.'

'Not only that,' her mother added, 'darling Lorenzo also had a long talk with James and he's persuaded him to stay on at the Hall—so lucky he and Mr Wilkins took to each other, wasn't it?'

'Wilkins and James ... here at the Hall?' Darcy looked at her in bewilderment.

Her mother laughed merrily. 'Darling, don't be silly. Lorenzo has arranged everything and we're moving out in two weeks' time. He is planning to pour workmen into this house and has promised me that when you return from your honeymoon trip to Sicily, all the alterations will be done and the Hall will be ready for you both to move in.' She smiled happily as she got up to make another pot of coffee.

Darcy tried to school her face into immobility as she fumed within. It was clear that 'darling Lorenzo' was the hero of the hour, here in Suffolk. Why in God's name hadn't her oh-so-wonderful husband bothered to tell her about all the arrangements he'd obviously been so busy organising? It was just like the damn man not to bother consulting her and it was certainly the first she'd heard about a honeymoon trip to Sicily!

Although being surprised at his actions only showed how stupid she was, Darcy told herself. Lorenzo was busy organising everything in sight for the sole reason that he couldn't wait to get into the house, the purchase of which had set the whole miserable farce of her marriage on its unhappy way. How could she have become so bound up in her extraordinary life with Lorenzo to have forgotten exactly why he had married her? Totally immersed in her unhappy thoughts, she looked up startled as James put his head around the door.

''Ullo Darcy. Cripes, you look grand—ever so lah-de-dah!' He laughed as she pulled a face and stuck her tongue out at him. 'You watch your manners my girl! countesses aren't supposed to do things like that. Now missus,' he said, turning to Mrs Talbot, 'come and give us a hand. I've got as far as the library and I dunno what books you was wanting to take with you.'

'Moving house is sheer, unadulterated hell,' Claire commented as her mother hurriedly left the room. 'Oh by the way, I don't think I've told you all my lovely news. Darling Roddy is hoping to get some leave from the bank in September, so we're going to have the wedding in London and then we'll be living in Boston. Roddy has found a sweet little house and . . . goodness, it's all so exciting!'

Darcy sighed inwardly, trying not to feel envious as Claire bubbled over with happiness.

'Honestly, Darcy you do look marvellous, and it isn't just the clothes,' Claire smiled. 'I've never seen you look so blooming—like a sleek and well-cherished cat! I do hope that you're happy.'

'Oh yes, deliriously happy—what else?' Darcy buried her face in her coffee cup ashamed at not being able to hide the unhappy note in her voice.

'But Darcy . . .' her sister regarded her with suddenly anxious eyes. 'I thought . . . I mean . . . I know that you love Lorenzo and so I thought . . .'

'I . . .? Love Lorenzo? I can't begin to think where you got such a far-fetched idea from,' Darcy replied bleakly, suddenly feeling overwhelmingly tired of the whole charade. 'If you think that I'm in a utopian state of happily married bliss—you must be out of your mind! You, my dear sister, are looking at the extremely well-dressed, but nevertheless burnt offering on the altar of yet another of dear Father's hopeless schemes!'

'Oh my God!' Claire blanched, her pale blue eyes looking at Darcy in acute distress. 'You . . . you mean you didn't want to marry Lorenzo?'

'*Want to marry him?*' She gave a harsh laugh. 'That was the last thing on my mind. I was merely going through a rehearsal for *your* wedding at the time—just in case you've forgotten!' She looked in astonishment as Claire's eyes began to fill with tears.

'For goodness sake, there's no need for you to take it so hard. I . . . it was silly of me to let myself go like

that. I do want to have a long talk with you later, but
do try and pull yourself together,' she pleaded urgently.
'I can hear Mother coming back and she mustn't know
how I feel. Promise you won't tell her?'

Nodding miserably, Claire made an effort to hide her
obvious unhappiness at Darcy's revelation about her
marriage as Mrs Talbot entered the room.

'Claire, I've just had Mrs Vernon on the phone.
She says that she knows you've got a mind like a
sieve, but this is the second time you've forgotten
that she's supposed to be taking the measurements for
your wedding dress! However, she says if you drive
over immediately, she'll fit you in between
appointments.'

'Oh crumbs—I completely forgot!' Claire leapt to her
feet. 'I must dash. It takes absolutely ages to get to
Ipswich these days—they've got the road up again! 'Bye
Darcy—see you later . . .' she called over her shoulder
as she ran out the door.

'Come back, Claire! I've got to talk to you, and . . .'
Darcy's voice faltered as she heard a car door bang and
the engine start up.

'You'll have to talk to her later, dear,' her mother
said soothingly as Darcy swore impatiently under her
breath. 'And that goes for me too, I'm afraid. I've got
so much packing to do that although I'd love to sit here
gossiping all day, I really must get on. Why don't you
see if there's anything you want from your bedroom
and then we can maybe have a quiet lunch together.'

Darcy sat on her old bed miserably hugging
'Threadbear', the teddy she'd been given on her third
birthday. She could feel tears of self-pity trickling down
her cheeks as she looked around at the shabby furniture
and faded chintz curtains. Lorenzo and his builders will
sweep all this away, she told herself with a deep pang of
regret; and after all who could blame them? There
wasn't a thing here that was worth preserving. It was
just that she had slept in this room since she was born

and it was all achingly familiar—a small spot of security now lost to her for ever.

Come on—stop snivelling! she railed at her weak, inner self. You can't sit here all day feeling sorry for yourself. Putting 'Threadbear' back on the bed, she went over to the dressing table to wipe her eyes and repair her make-up before going downstairs.

Darcy found her mother sorting out yet more china in the pantry. 'I . . . er . . . I don't think I'll stay to lunch. I may as well drive over to Cambridge and sort out my things at the flat.'

'That sounds a good idea, darling,' her mother answered abstractedly. 'Now where was I? Six . . . no, eight soup bowls and . . .' Darcy smiled wryly and left Mrs Talbot to her packing.

So much for my plan to have a long talk with Claire, she thought despondently as she drove through the narrow streets of Cambridge. She was going to call at her old flat, of course, but what she really intended to do was to have a long talk with Richard Petrie. Surely his clever brain would be able to think of a way for her to wriggle out of the entanglement in which she found herself?

However, by the time she was on the road back to London, Darcy knew that she had reached her nadir, the very lowest point of her existence so far. At least when she had been told she was married, she had been positive that she could find some way of escape. Now all hope was gone.

Her flatmate Sally had been delighted to see her, although puzzled as to why Darcy was concerned over her books. Surely she hadn't forgotten that her husband had arranged for everything to be put in storage? The removal men had been three days ago, and Lorenzo had sent Sally a cheque for six months' rent, which would mean that she didn't have to rush to find someone to take Darcy's place. Wasn't it kind of him?

Feeling almost sick with frustration, Darcy had

found Richard in his college rooms, his nose buried in a weighty volume. It was with some difficulty that she persuaded him to put it down and listen to the account of her troubles.

'Can't see what you expect me to do, Darcy?' He blinked owlishly at her. 'Your husband called to see me the other day. Don't know why he bothered, though. Nice chap, good brain too. Knew a lot about chemistry. That's it really,' he added, his eyes straying longingly back to his book.

Darcy had looked at him for a long moment before getting up to leave. 'Why did I never realise what a ... a spineless idiot you were, Richard? *Absolutely spineless!*' she shouted, banging the door behind her as hard as she could.

Returning the hired car to its garage, Darcy walked slowly back through the evening rush hour crowds to the Barbican. Her head throbbed, pounding with the realisation that with masterly precision Lorenzo had cut off all lines of retreat, leaving her no alternative but to remain tied to him for the foreseeable future. She could run away, of course—but where to? And even if she did, she knew that her hateful husband would manage to find her—somehow.

'Ah, I was wondering where you were.' Lorenzo looked sternly up at her from behind his desk as she entered the apartment.

'Were you?' she answered dully.

Gazing at her weary, drooping figure, his eyes softened. 'Why do you not go and have a long, hot bath?' he suggested in a kinder tone of voice. 'I will arrange for us to have a quiet meal here in the apartment tonight, so there is no need to hurry.'

Darcy shrugged and with leaden feet made her way to the bedroom.

It wasn't until dinner was almost over that night that she felt able to broach the subject of her visit to Belmont Hall, although there was no way she was ever going to let him know about her visit to Richard Petrie. She still felt far too raw and humiliated by Richard's lack of interest in her to do that.

'You didn't tell me that you had flown up to see my parents,' she said, her lips tight with annoyance.

'Ah, so that was where you were . . .' Lorenzo smiled lazily. 'Did I not, *cara?* It must have escaped my mind, that is all. Would you care for a liqueur?' he asked as Wilkins brought in the coffee.

Darcy waited until they were alone again, before returning to the attack. 'Has it also escaped your mind that you are handling the purchase of a house for my parents? You would appear to have a bad case of amnesia about our so-called honeymoon trip to Sicily as well!'

'No,' he answered, his lips twitching with amusement. 'I . . . er . . . I think that I can just remember those items.'

'Great! In that case, maybe you can tell me how my father and mother can possibly afford a house like that? I may not have been in London for very long,' she added sharply, 'but even I know that a house in that area of London is going to cost far more money than they will have left from the sale of Belmont Hall.'

'Very true,' he agreed with maddening calm. 'You must try one of these peaches, *cara,* they are delicious.' He passed her the bowl of fruit.

'Oh—damn the peaches!' she swore impatiently. 'I want to know what's going on?'

Lorenzo sighed and sat back in his chair. 'You have made it quite obvious that you actively dislike this apartment. Since I expect my proposed takeover to be completed by the end of this week, I decided that you would prefer to holiday in Sicily while the alterations to your old home are carried out. Of course, if you would prefer to stay here in London . . .?'

Darcy flushed with annoyance beneath his sardonically amused expression. 'No . . . well, I . . .'

'Precisely,' he commented dryly. 'As far as your parents are concerned, Darcy, it is very simple. To put it crudely, your father is an improvident wastrel who will, I imagine, soon go through all the money he has received for Belmont Hall. By buying a house in London and putting it in your mother's name, I am merely providing for her comfortable old age. Surely you approve of that?'

'Yes, of course. But . . .'

'The choice of location was deliberate. It is very central and when either of her daughters wishes to see her—one is going to be living in America I understand—access to central London is easier than anywhere else I can think of. Besides which, your father will hand to me a sum which I will tell him is to pay for the new house. That money will be sensibly invested to bring in a small but adequate annuity for your mother so that she may never want for the small luxuries of life.'

Lorenzo watched the conflicting expressions chase themselves across his wife's lovely face. 'It is merely a sensible arrangement, hmm?'

'Yes, I . . .' Darcy struggled to appear grateful. Which of course she was, she told herself, only . . . 'You're taking over possession of the whole family!' she burst out angrily. 'First our home, then . . . then me and now . . .' she gestured helplessly as he continued to smile lazily at her confusion.

'I do not recall that you have been protesting too loudly at my . . . er . . . possession *cara*,' he purred softly. 'Certainly not for the last week, if my memory serves me correctly, hmm?'

'Oh—go to hell!' she ground out through clenched teeth, jumping up and running over to look blindly out of the large open window.

'And leave you all alone in our large bed? Ah no, Darcy, you cannot make me believe that you do not enjoy being a woman in my arms.' His voice was hateful in its mocking cynicism as he came over to stand beside her.

'That's . . . well, it's just lust. All that you've proved is that you're an . . . an accomplished seducer and that I'm . . .' she gave a muffled sob. 'I'm just a weak woman—that's all.'

'Ah no. You are much, much more than that,' he whispered, bending to gently place his lips against the back of her neck beside the heavy knot of golden hair.

A nervous shiver iced its way down her spine and she suddenly felt an almost insane urge to turn and lift her face for his kiss. Breathlessly she fought against such a treacherous desire for the touch of the man she so disliked, trembling as he slipped a strong arm about her waist and trailed a gentle finger down the delicate curve of her cheek. His mouth followed the path of his finger, his lips moving over hers softly and lightly, so that her own quivered and parted as he began a gentle exploration of such an aching sweetness that when he drew away she had an oddly perverse feeling of regret.

Time seemed to be suspended as she gazed bemusedly up into his dark gleaming eyes before he gave a soft, low laugh and swept her up into his arms, carrying her with effortless ease towards their bedroom.

And that, Darcy thought bitterly as she gazed out of the aeroplane, that had been the pattern of her and Lorenzo's relationship since their marriage. No matter how hard she steeled herself during the day, no amount of firm resolution and determined, well-planned obduracy had any effect once Lorenzo placed his arms about her body.

Night after night there was no reprieve, no surcease from his passionate lovemaking. At first she had fought wildly, like one possessed. The only result of such exertion on her part had been his low growl of amusement and a contemptuous disregard of the struggling, protesting figure in his arms as his hands and mouth had worked their devilish magic.

After the first few nights, however, it had been ... well, different. Somehow there had seemed to be little point in screaming and raging when the end result was always the same. Maybe it was because she had finally resigned herself to her fate, she told herself hurriedly. Maybe that was the reason why she had become such a pliant, willing slave to Lorenzo's seemingly inexhaustible desire for her body?

Darcy opened her handbag, feverishly hunting for a handkerchief to hide her flushed cheeks as Lorenzo, who had been chatting to the pilot, came back to sit down beside her.

'Now, Darcy, when we land the stewardess will hand you a bouquet which she has been keeping cool in the galley. She will also hand you a small circlet of flowers which I wish you to wear on your head.' He raised a warning hand as she opened her mouth to refute such an idiotic suggestion.

'Please listen to what I say. I know you have been irritated by having to wear what you regard as an unsuitable dress, but the people of my estate will wish to give a traditional welcome to my bride and I am merely outfitting you in accordance with their expectations.'

'But I'll feel such a fool! I mean ... it all sounds so ridiculously feudal and ...'

'In many ways Sicily is a feudal country, *cara*. I am asking you to just trust me and to do as I say, hmm?'

Having no alternative but to reluctantly agree to his request, Darcy sat stiff with embarrassment as the large black car which had met them at Palermo airport climbed the tortuous mountain road.

'I feel like some crazy Queen of the May,' she groaned, gesturing to the small circle of pink and white roses on top of her hair which lay in a long, golden stream down her back.

'No. You look very lovely, my darling. Very lovely indeed.'

Darcy could feel her cheeks flush at the husky tone of his voice and turned her head to look out of the window. 'My goodness,' she gasped suddenly. 'Is that a cable car?'

'Yes, it provides a much quicker journey up and down the mountain, but I thought that for this occasion a limousine would be more . . . er . . . dignified.'

Darcy couldn't repress a small gurgle of laughter as she pictured herself swaying around in the air, dressed as a bride.

'That is better. I am always desolated when you are cross with me.' His voice was heavy with mock sorrow as he raised her hand to his lips.

'Oh yeah!' she snorted vulgarly, colouring beneath the gleam in his dark eyes as he threw back his head and roared with laughter.

'Oh, my Darcy—what a wife I have married!'

'Well, I did warn you at the time that I wouldn't suit you, so you've only yourself to blame!'

'On the contrary—you suit me very well. Especially at night, yes?' he added softly.

'No!' she muttered angrily, averting her burning face from his gaze.

'You are a shockingly bad liar!' He laughed as the car came to a halt in the middle of a town square. Darcy, preoccupied with her confused emotions, looked in bewilderment at the packed crowds of people who cheered and shouted as Lorenzo opened his door and came around to help her alight.

Hanging tightly on to Lorenzo's arm, she found herself walking slowly through the square and up the narrow street which led to a castle, which like the small town seemed to be perched on top of the mountain. The bystanders parted to let them through calling out in Italian and showering them with nuts and corn.

'They are wishing us much joy and praying that our marriage will be fruitful,' Lorenzo explained as Darcy, feeling warmed and touched, smiled shyly back at the friendly, laughing faces.

Approaching the great Norman arch of the gatehouse which fronted the steep walls of the castle, she saw that a group of people were awaiting their arrival. A man stepped forward with a pottery bowl. 'Welcome, Excellency, welcome to your house,' he said, placing the bowl into Lorenzo's hands.

'It is wine, and we must both now spill it on the ground before we enter the castle,' he explained. Mystified, Darcy placed her hands on the bowl as directed and then watched with interest as having spilt the wine, Lorenzo threw the bowl on the ground where it broke into tiny pieces.

There was a loud murmur of satisfaction at his action from the crowd behind them as he led Darcy inside the castle, passing servants carrying cakes and wine towards the people in the square.

'Ah, Lorenzo. Welcome!' A slim, elderly man hurried forward with a beaming smile.

'Darcy, I wish you to meet my uncle Vito, my father was his elder brother.'

'Your bride is lovely.' Uncle Vito smiled happily at Darcy as Lorenzo introduced a plump, middle-aged woman as his uncle's wife, Paola.

Still feeling somewhat overwhelmed by their reception in the town square, she followed Aunt Paola into the great hall of the castle, gasping with delight at her surroundings. The late afternoon sun poured in through the tall mullioned windows spotlighting the brilliant jewel-like colours of the family banners which hung suspended from brass rods high up on the great rough-hewn stone walls, rising in sombre magnificence to the high, vaulted ceiling way above her head.

Smiling with pleasure, Darcy turned to Lorenzo's aunt who was twisting a handkerchief in her hands and casting nervous, apprehensive glances at Lorenzo. Following the woman's gaze, she saw from his stern expression that all was not well.

'Where is Adriana?' he demanded. 'Why is she not here to greet my wife?'

Uncle Vito, rolling his eyes nervously in his wife's direction, replied in heavily accented English that Adriana was upstairs in her bedroom.

'Fetch her down here. Immediately!' Lorenzo's sharp command sent his aunt scurrying out of the room, leaving Darcy and his uncle to stand in awkward silence while Lorenzo waited with ill-concealed impatience for his order to be obeyed.

Darcy felt totally bewildered. What had gone wrong? Who on earth was Adriana and why all the fuss?

After some minutes Aunt Paola reappeared, leading forward a small, petite girl of perhaps sixteen or seventeen whose extraordinary beauty was temporarily marred by a ferocious scowl.

'*Allora, Adriana . . .?*' Darcy couldn't follow the rapid exchange of Italian between Lorenzo and the girl, but it was plain to see that they weren't exchanging pleasantries as they talked quickly and angrily to each other. There was a sudden silence as Lorenzo's face became hard and stern. When he spoke it was in English and his words were terrifyingly direct.

'I am not prepared to have any nonsense from you, Adriana. You will now greet my wife formally, politely and with due humility as befits her rank. *Ha capito?*'

Darcy stared fixedly down, wishing with all her heart that she could vanish through the grey marble floor. What did it matter whether the girl had been here to meet them or not? She, for one, couldn't care less— anything was better than this dreadful scene.

'*Subito*, Adriana! At once!' Lorenzo thundered, the suppressed rage in his voice bouncing off the stone walls of the large hall.

Adriana shrugged a delicate shoulder and came over

to stand in front of Darcy who smiled nervously into her lovely face. With downcast eyes Adriana mumbled something in Italian before flashing a piercing look of hatred at the English girl and running out of the room.

'*Va bene,*' Lorenzo grunted. 'You will please go with my aunt, Darcy. She will show you to our rooms while I see to the luggage.'

If she thought that the scene in the hall was a bad start to a holiday, the dinner which followed was infinitely worse. Darcy sat in embarrassed silence as Lorenzo roundly condemned the state of the castle, 'Dust everywhere, Aunt Paola'; the standard of service, 'I will not tolerate sloppy servants'; and the food, 'I haven't tasted veal as tough as this in a long time.' All of which, Darcy thought, was very unfair, having found the whole meal absolutely delicious. She was just trying to summon up enough courage to put forward an opposing view, when Lorenzo cleared his throat and called for silence.

'I am now going to speak very plainly, so I suggest that you all listen very carefully.' He looked around the table. 'As a family we are proud of our long line of descent from the Norman Kings who once ruled this country. I wish to inform you that my wife has an equally long pedigree—probably longer. If therefore she is not treated with all *respect* as is due to my wife, I shall have to ask you all to leave this castle. Have I made myself entirely clear?'

Lorenzo stood up and in the dreadful silence which followed his words, he walked slowly down the room to stand by Darcy's chair. 'Please remember that I must and will have *respect* for my wife—or you will all be very sorry. Come Darcy, I think it is time we retired.'

There was no sound except the click of her heels as he led her nervous, trembling figure from the room, and it wasn't until he shut the door of their suite that she was able to find her voice.

'You ... you were perfectly beastly and horrid to

your family!' she cried. 'Your poor aunt and uncle!
Why . . . why did you have to drag me into it all? How
on earth do you expect them to be friends with me after
. . . after what you said . . .' She waved her hands
distractedly in the air.

'Calm down, Darcy.' Lorenzo came over from a
cupboard in the corner and placed a glass of whisky in
her hands. 'My family and I are Sicilian and we all
understand each other perfectly! I was merely sorting
out the ground rules for our stay here, that is all.
Everyone now knows, without doubt, exactly what I
expect from them and you will find that your holiday
will be very pleasant.'

'I'm glad you think so . . .' she muttered grimly.

'I know so!'

'But why did you go on about the house and the food
and . . . and all that nonsense about me?' she looked at
him in bewilderment.

'The English have an expression "when the cat's
away the mice will play", yes?' He grinned. 'Since I
know that my words will be repeated in the servants'
hall and down in the town, I am merely reminding
everyone that I am back in residence. And if,' he
laughed, 'if you are going to tell me that I am behaving
like a feudal overlord, you are quite right, I am! If I did
not, I would be despised as a weak man of no account.'

He sipped his drink and looked at her reflectively.
'This is a different country and way of life to that which
you are used to, Darcy. "Respect" is something that is
very important here. It would take a lifetime for me to
try and explain all the nuances of my speech tonight. I
suggest that we now both forget it and go to bed,
hmm?'

'But I . . .'

'Oh Dio, Dio!' Lorenzo groaned as he walked over
and took her roughly into his arms. 'Don't tell me that
I'm going to have to shout at you as well, cara?'

Darcy felt suddenly breathless, her heart beginning to

thud as she glimpsed the naked desire in the dark eyes gleaming down at her so intently. Leaning weakly against his broad chest, savouring the heat of his body through his thin silk shirt, she trembled as his hands began to caress the soft swell of her hips.

'Ah . . . I am glad to see that at least my wife seems to know what is good for her!' he murmured with a low laugh, reaching up to slowly undo her zip . . .

CHAPTER EIGHT

DARCY poured herself another cup of coffee, sitting back to gaze through the open window at the magnificent view which lay spread out before her. In the foreground, below the sheer precipitous drop from the castle which was perched on the highest point of the mountain, lay the coastal town of Trapani, whose white salt pans were dazzling in the early morning sun, while in the distance she could just make out the shadowy coastline of North Africa. Sighing with contentment, she closed her eyes and savoured the soft morning breeze, whose rising air currents carried the sharp scent of pines from the valley below.

Lorenzo was right, she thought lazily. Her holiday was indeed proving to be very pleasant—almost blissful in fact. She couldn't possibly have imagined that in just over one week she would have become completely enchanted with both Sicily and also the Castello Tancredi, the ancient Norman castle that was Lorenzo's ancestral home.

Every morning Lorenzo had flown down by helicopter to the port of Gela, the centre of his petrochemical empire, leaving her to have a lazy breakfast here in the sitting room of their suite before setting out to explore the castle. The clattering noise of the returning helicopter as it landed in a courtyard on the far side of the castle was the general signal that the midday meal would soon be ready. No one would dare to serve lunch before he returned, Darcy thought with a wry smile. They were all much too frightened of him.

The dramatic and forceful way Lorenzo had chosen to reassert his authority on their first evening in the castle seemed to have produced the required results, if servants fleeing at his approach or trembling as they bowed to the ground in his presence, was what he intended. For her part, Darcy felt that she could have done with a little less of the 'respect' that he seemed to feel was so important. She had tried to thank one of the maids who had brought in her breakfast tray this morning, but all she could elicit from the girl had been a hurriedly muttered, *'Chiedo scusa, Contessa'* and a scared look as she had scuttled from the room.

She couldn't sit here all day in her dressing gown, she told herself, looking with pleasure at the bright tapestries which covered the old stone walls. Stretching lazily in the morning sunshine, she winced at a slight stiffness in her neck. Lorenzo had taken her to see over the Palazzo dei Normanni in Palermo yesterday afternoon. She remembered that she had craned her head back so far to look up at the magnificent wooden ceiling in the Palatine Chapel, that he had laughingly told her to watch out that she didn't fall over.

Their relationship had subtly altered since their arrival in Sicily. It was of course scorchingly hot, and when she had insisted on wearing light cotton summer dresses with bare legs and sandals, he had surprisingly raised no objection. He had asked that she should dress more formally at night, but that was no problem as she had brought several light, filmy evening dresses with her.

It wasn't just the clothes, of course ... Ever since they had left England he had been more friendly and certainly more relaxed. It was rare for him to issue his usual peremptory orders—to her at any rate—and there were other changes that had occurred. It wasn't only Lorenzo who had altered ...

Darcy could feel her cheeks burning as she recalled how their lovemaking had changed, how wantonly and with what abandon she now responded to his touch. She moved restlessly in her chair as she remembered the piercing sweetness of their passionate encounter last night.

Darcy's thoughts were interrupted by a knock and she looked up, her face still flushed from the recollection of Lorenzo's lovemaking, to see Aunt Paola enter the room bearing a large, heavy wooden box.

'I am not disturbing you . . .' she asked hesitantly.

'Oh no, please come in. I've been disgracefully lazy, just sitting here and enjoying the morning sunshine.'

'*Va bene.* I am very sorry not to have brought this to you before now,' she nodded down at the box in her hands. 'Unfortunately it had been put away in the bank and I needed Lorenzo's signature to release it.'

'What is it? I don't understand.' She looked down in puzzlement at the box which Aunt Paola had placed in her lap.

'Open it. Open it and you will see.'

Darcy's slim fingers had difficulty in prising open the heavy brass lock, the rusty hinges creaking in protest as she lifted the lid. 'Oh no! I can't possibly . . . I mean . . .' she gasped, staring in stupefaction at the contents.

'*Si, si.* But yes, of course. As my nephew's wife it is yours.' Aunt Paola lifted out the velvet-lined tray on which lay a magnificent diamond and ruby necklace, together with a matching bracelet and earrings. 'See, here and here . . .!'

Darcy's eyes grew round in amazement as the older woman continued to remove five more trays containing an assortment of jewellery, the like of which she had never seen before. Earrings, bracelets and necklaces fashioned from precious stones sparkled in the sun as Aunt Paola spread the trays out on the table.

Darcy shook her head in confusion. 'It's an incredible collection. I couldn't possibly wear any of it, of course, but . . .' she peered down, 'aren't some of the pieces very old?'

'Oh yes,' Lorenzo's aunt sighed with pleasure as she carefully lifted up what appeared to be a wide, flat neckband made of solid gold. The four large, smoothly rounded rubies embedded in the gold gave off a deep blood-red glow, very different from the more modern cut of some of the other precious stones on the trays.

'It's lovely, but it must be a very uncomfortable necklace to wear, surely?'

'But no!' Aunt Paola looked at her with shocked eyes as she turned the neckband over in her hands. 'You see? It is a diadem—a crown to be worn by a woman. It is very precious to our family because it is said to have belonged to Queen Sibylla, the wife of King Tancred.'

Darcy sat looking at the tiara-like object which Aunt Paola had placed in her hands, trying to remember the line of Norman kings which had ruled Sicily in approximately the same time in history as the Norman conquest of England. That had been the golden age of Sicily when, for the first and only time in history, the European, Islamic and Byzantine peoples had lived harmoniously together, before the Norman line had virtually died out and the island had fallen into the hands of the German Emperors.

Tancred had been the last Norman king, she remembered, ruling for only four years before dying of some disease at the relatively early age of forty-five.

'But surely King Tancred only had two sons, one that died before his father and the other, a young boy, who died later in captivity? I've never been able to understand how Lorenzo and your husband could claim to have been his descendants?'

'Ah, no. It is said that when Queen Sibylla fled to take refuge from the German invader, she was pregnant. She had a baby boy, which she left hidden behind in Caltabellotta when she was forced to attend the new King's coronation before she was sent to captivity in Germany.'

Aunt Paola's earnest explanation wasn't entirely convincing, Darcy mused, her analytical historian's brain rapidly reviewing the possible truth of an event which had taken place so long ago. It would have been a miracle if such a royal birth had taken place undetected. No, it was much more likely that Lorenzo's family were descended from a bastard son of the King, although she wouldn't dream of destroying Aunt Paola's illusions! During the last week Darcy had become very fond of Lorenzo's aunt and uncle, who had both proved to be very friendly and helpful.

'The jewellery is lovely,' she said as she replaced the tiara back on its tray. 'But I really can't accept it.'

'Lorenzo will insist that you do so, and as you know, my dear, that will be that!'

Looking at the twinkle in Aunt Paola's eyes, Darcy gave a rueful grin in acknowledgment of Lorenzo's ruthless determination to have his own way. 'Yes, I expect he will. Still, it is all far too valuable to be worn except on the grandest occasions, so maybe the question will not arise. Honestly, I've never seen anything like it.'

'Do your family not have such a collection?' Aunt Paola asked as Darcy bent down to replace the trays in the box.

'Goodness no!' Darcy giggled. 'I don't think the Talbots have ever had a penny to their name, let alone a collection of jewels like these!'

'Talbot . . .? Is that a common surname in England?' Aunt Paola asked, looking down startled at Darcy's bowed head.

Darcy shrugged. 'I really don't know, not very I shouldn't have thought. My family has lived in the same house—Belmont Hall, which Lorenzo has just bought—for the last five hundred years. But I expect there are lots of other Talbots around the country . . .' She glanced up. 'Aunt Paola—for Heaven's sake! Are you all right?' she cried in concern as the older woman slumped down in a chair, her face as white as a sheet.

'Yes, I . . . it's nothing, really. I sometimes have turns like this, I will be all right in a minute.'

Darcy ran into the bathroom to get a glass of water, and after taking a few sips the colour seemed to come back into Aunt Paola's face.

'You really ought to see a doctor, you know.'

'Yes, I will. Please don't worry, I feel much better already. I . . . er . . . I have been meaning to say to you Darcy that I am sorry about . . . about Adriana's rudeness to you over the last week. It is just that she is very young and . . .'

'Please! It doesn't matter a bit. I'm much more concerned that you should go and lie down, you didn't look at all well just now.'

'You are a good, kind girl, Darcy. Very kind . . .' Aunt Paola sighed heavily as she rose and walked slowly out of the room.

Poor Aunt Paola, Darcy thought as she went into the bedroom to get dressed. It was nice of her to try and apologise for Adriana who wasn't just rude—she was impossible! Nothing Darcy said or did seemed to be able to reconcile Adriana to Lorenzo's marriage. She had absolutely no idea why the young girl should hate her so fiercely, why at every opportunity she was rude, spiteful and aggressive.

Maybe she was going through a particularly trying period of adolescence, Darcy mused, trying to remember herself at the age of seventeen. The only picture she could conjure up was of a quiet, studious girl with her nose always firmly pressed into a book; simply light years away from the sultry, ripe and obviously sexually aware Adriana.

Slipping into a pale blue sleeveless cotton dress, Darcy coiled her hair into a loose knot at the back of her neck and after swiftly checking her appearance in the mirror she left the suite to wander slowly down the corridor towards a spiral staircase which led up into the library tower. The problem of Adriana still occupied her mind. It was probably her parents' fault that she was so unruly and aggressive, Darcy realised. However, it was difficult to blame Uncle Vito and Aunt Paola too much. Like a pair of plain, homely and rather timid birds they regarded their daughter very much as if she was some outstandingly beautiful cuckoo who had been unaccountably placed in their nest, treating her with a mixture of nervous bewilderment and apprehensive pride.

All thought of Adriana and her parents, of the castle and even of Lorenzo left her mind as she reached the library, a room of whose existence she hadn't known until she discovered it yesterday. With sparkling eyes and a nose that twitched like that of a hound on the scent of a fox, she slipped inside and closed the door quietly behind her.

Darcy nearly jumped out of her skin as the library door was thrown open with a bang. She looked up startled to see Lorenzo, his face as black as thunder, standing in the doorway.

'*Mannaggia!*' he growled. 'I hope you realise that it is now two o'clock and that the whole castle has been turned upside down for the last hour—just looking for you!'

Darcy quailed beneath his fury. 'I'm . . . I'm sorry. I had no idea that it was so late, really I didn't. It was just that I . . .' She shrugged helplessly as she looked down at the pile of vellum manuscripts and old leather books on the table before her.

'I might have known that you would have found your way to this room!' he snorted in exasperation.

'I'm terribly sorry to have got so immersed in these books and kept everybody waiting, but it's been so interesting—you've no idea! I mean, there's this really old manuscript copy of *Historia Sicula* by someone called Geoffrey Malaterra. It's all in a mixture of Latin and old Norman French, of course, but I can just understand it and . . .'

'Enough—enough!' He raised his hands, his mouth twisted wryly, as he gazed down into her sparkling blue eyes. 'I can see that I have lost you to the dust of history, and that it will always be so. Hmm?'

'I can't help it, Lorenzo, although I don't suppose you can possibly understand. It's just that . . .'

'It's just that, for you, the past is more important than the present. Oh yes, unfortunately I do understand, Darcy. I understand only too well!' Lorenzo's voice was harsh, his expression suddenly bleak and forbidding as he turned abruptly away to look at the shelves of leather-bound books. 'Come, we must not keep the family waiting any longer for their meal.'

Darcy's eyes were clouded with confusion as she accompanied his tall figure down the corridor towards the dining room. It was, of course, annoying of her to have become so immersed in the manuscripts she had found. However, as she peeped up through her eyelashes at his stern, strained face, she was at a loss to understand why he should be so ... well, so angry at having found her in the library. Why should he care one way or another?

Although, mercifully, Adriana was absent, the atmosphere at lunch was clouded by Lorenzo's monosyllabic answers to any remarks addressed to him by Uncle Vito and Aunt Paola, and his general air of gloomy abstraction. Maybe he had some pressing problems in the factories, Darcy thought, staring idly up at the painting of his mother, which accompanied other old family portraits on the wood panelled walls.

Lorenzo certainly didn't take after his mother. A point she had made to Aunt Paola on being given a short conducted tour of the castle's main rooms yesterday.

'Helena was so lovely, so *simpatico*, but she was very ill at the time, you understand. She only agreed to be painted because Lorenzo wished it so much.' Aunt Paola sighed heavily as they both stood looking into the blue eyes of the woman whose faded blonde hair and pain-etched face still held the traces of a past beauty.

'*Povera donna*,' Aunt Paola had murmured, sighing again. 'Poor woman, she died when her son was only sixteen. Helena had been ill for a long time, but always she said she must stay alive to continue looking after the business until Lorenzo was old enough to take over.

So sad not to see his success. So very sad.'

Gazing now at the portrait, Darcy felt a pang of sorrow for a woman who had died at such an early age. How shattering it must have been for her son to find himself all alone at the age of sixteen . . .

She turned to look at Lorenzo and saw that he was deep in quiet conversation with Aunt Paola. The older woman seemed to be trying to emphasise the importance of something, becoming extremely agitated when Lorenzo shook his head in curt disagreement as he rose from the table.

'Come,' he said taking her hand firmly in his. 'I wish to see you privately.'

'Oh Lord, what have I done now?' she asked apprehensively as he issued her into their suite.

'Done? Absolutely nothing as far as I know. I am only interested in *what* you are going to do, my Darcy.'

She looked up in sudden alarm at the harsh, thick note in his voice as he seized her hand and began to lead her into the bedroom. 'Lorenzo! You . . . surely you can't . . .'

'Oh, yes I can! Do you doubt it, *cara*?'

Her heart began to race at the fiercely dark, mocking gleam in his eyes. 'But . . . it's only the middle of the afternoon, for Heaven's sake!'

'Ah, my dear wife—how very prim and proper you pretend to be!' His hoarse whisper sent shivers tingling down her spine as he removed the pins and let loose her long, golden hair. 'But we both know better, don't we?'

She stood as one turned to stone, mesmerised by the terrifying implacability of his hawk-like features as he swiftly ripped the clothes from her body and tossed her on to the bed with consummate ease. For a moment she lay dazed and winded before struggling to sit up as he rapidly divested himself of his clothing.

'Oh, no . . . no!' she gasped, suddenly frightened by a glimpse of the raging desire in his eyes as his hard body moved to pin her trembling figure to the mattress.

'*Ma si!* What has the time or the hour to do with making love?' he queried savagely, before his mouth descended to cover hers with determined, bruising force.

This . . . this isn't making love . . . she wanted to scream, slipping beneath the waves of some deep, dark ocean as the brutal assault on her senses seemed almost unending; not this ruthless, savage plunder which ravaged her very soul. It was almost as if Lorenzo was being driven by a force he couldn't control, a ferocious hunger and tormenting thirst that could only be satisfied by his total possession of the slender body writhing so helplessly beneath him.

Afterwards, as she lay sobbing in his arms, he gently wiped the tears from her eyes, murmuring soft endearments until her storm of weeping ceased.

'Forgive me, my sweet one. *Oh Dio, Dio*—please forgive me. I . . .' he shook his head in bewilderment. 'I don't know what can have possessed me to do such a terrible, terrible thing,' he groaned with remorse. '*O Cristo . . .!*'

Almost without thought she turned and gently wound her slim arms about his trembling body, placing his head on her breast and cradling him like a small child as she lay staring blindly up at the ceiling.

What . . . what's happening to me, she thought in confusion. Surely she should hate this man who had just subjected her to such an unforgivably ruthless assault? How could she be lying here rocking him tenderly in her arms, her heart torn with pity and compassion at the unknown, dark forces which had impelled him to behave in the way he had?

Drowsily she watched the particles of dust dancing in the beam of sunlight which flooded in through the large window, the thin voile curtains billowing in the light breeze. With sleepy dismay she tried to shut her tired mind to the logical conclusion her sub-conscious brain was thrusting upon her. Love him? Of course not! The idea was simply too preposterous to even think about, she firmly told herself as she fell asleep.

Darcy leant against the rough stone wall of the high watch tower, looking over the ramparts as the fiery red ball of the sun slowly slipped down over the horizon, seeming to turn the Egadi Islands which lay offshore into dark ships sailing on an ocean that the dying sun had turned to fire.

It was almost as if her extraordinary relationship with Lorenzo had reached a watershed on that hot afternoon, Darcy thought, looking back over the past ten days. Cautiously and hesitantly, he had slowly relaxed his guard, allowing her glimpses of a softer character, an inner warmth beneath the hard, forceful and ruthless personality with which he normally faced the world.

Even Aunt Paola had blinked in amazement as, despite his business commitments, he had taken Darcy out every day to visit the many ancient sights and old buildings on the island, all of which he must have seen hundreds of times before. He had even—rather heroically she thought, remembering the tiring journey by car, cable car and then on foot—escorted her to the summit of Mount Etna, whose fiercely bubbling lava deep in the volcanic crater had been an unforgettable sight.

And the nights. The nights they spent locked in each other's arms had been magical ones of such aching sweetness that many times she had almost wept with joy.

It had taken her two days of fierce, constant arguments with herself before she had been forced to acknowledge that somehow, somewhere between her original masquerade as Claire and her holiday on this enchanted island, she had fallen deeply and irrevocably in love with her husband.

Maybe it was the hot, searing heat of the sun, the

humid atmosphere of the long summer days, but she seemed wrapped in a languorous and fatalistic acceptance of her fate, something she could never have contemplated in London. Although reason told her that she was living in a fool's paradise, that she was only one of a long line of women who had fallen victim to Lorenzo's charm, she had no desire or will to do anything other than love and cherish him with all her heart.

With a click the tower was flooded with light and she turned startled as she heard footsteps approaching up the spiral stone staircase.

'I thought I would find you up here. It was also my mother's favourite place at this time of the evening,' Lorenzo added with a warm smile as he walked across the grey flagstones. Placing a glass of wine in her hand, he came to stand beside her, gazing out at the panoramic view of mountains, plains, sea and sky which lay spread out before them.

'I've never . . . well, I've never liked to ask you about your parents, Lorenzo. Do you miss them very much?' she asked gently.

He shrugged his broad shoulders. 'I can hardly remember my father, *cara*. He died in a storm at sea when I was seven—a long time ago. But of course I miss my mother very much. She had a hard life in many ways, and I only wish that she was alive now so that I could look after her,' he sipped his drink. 'Ah well, life is full of regrets, no?'

Darcy, who had caught the note of pain behind his last careless words, looked searchingly at his autocratic profile as he stared out over the wall at the magnificent sunset.

'Please tell me about your mother. I . . . I would like to know something about her.'

He hesitated for a moment as if gathering his thoughts. 'She was English, like you, Darcy. After what I imagine to have been a fairly uneventful childhood, she met my father on holiday one year, and despite her parents' objections and disapproval—she married him. Her family refused to have anything more to do with her after that.'

'Oh, I'm sorry, Lorenzo . . .'

'Yes, so was she,' he added dryly. 'She told me that she had always got on with her older brother, but he was killed in the war, and very soon after she was married, her parents, who were quite elderly, died within a short time of each other.'

'Was she very lonely out here—not having any family of her own, I mean?'

'She and my father were very happy together. Our family may be an old one, but after Mussolini came to power in Italy, much of our land was confiscated since my grandfather refused to join the Fascists. My father very sensibly left politics strictly alone and became involved in building up a small fleet of tankers. While he was certainly no Onassis, he was very well off when he died. Very far from the "poor fisherman" to which her parents objected.'

'Aunt Paola said something about your mother keeping the business going when you were young?' she murmured tentatively.

'Yes, just! To start with, anyway. Several of my father's competitors made her "offers she couldn't refuse".' He smiled wryly at the surprise on Darcy's face. 'You must not forget that Sicily is the homeland of the Mafia. Which is the main reason why I don't live here permanently—but that is by the by. Suffice to say that my mother by a mixture of charm and low English cunning, managed to keep the business going and the wolves at bay,' he chuckled. 'When I was sixteen, I took the business over and matters developed from then on.'

'It must have been very hard for her to do everything on her own. Couldn't Uncle Vito or someone else have helped her?'

Lorenzo laughed. 'My darling girl, you surely must

see that dear Uncle Vito is hardly a rock on which one could lean, charming man though he is. No, after she was rebuffed by her brother, she did all she had to do on her own.'

Darcy looked at him with a puzzled frown. 'But you said her brother was dead, at least that's what I thought you said . . .'

'Yes, I . . .' he paused for a moment. 'I mentioned her elder brother, but she also had a younger brother. When my father died she . . . er . . . she wrote to him, telling him that she had a small child and also about her . . . er . . . various difficulties.'

'What did he do to help her?' Darcy found herself caught up in the story.

'Do? Well, he didn't do *nothing*, of course. No, that would have been the action of a man who didn't care about his sister one way or another. He, in fact, felt very strongly about her. So strongly that he had his solicitors reply to her letter, informing her that her action in marrying my father had not only killed his parents, but the disgrace had also blighted his own career as a cavalry officer in one of the best regiments, and that he wished for no further communication.'

'Oh my God—how awful! Your poor mother, how she must have suffered,' Darcy's warm heart was wrung with love and tenderness for Lorenzo, who still obviously carried the scars of his mother's treatment by her family.

'I think that she was too busy, and having to work too hard, to care very much one way or another. In fact it was I who for years burned for revenge against the injustice of her family's rejection. Now,' he shrugged, 'now it no longer seems very important to me.'

'Well, I think it was disgraceful! It was very shabby indeed of her brother to treat his sister in such a way— really awful in fact.'

'It all happened a long time ago, *cara*. Far more

important is the fact that I have suddenly realised that I am hungry.'

'Well, I'll have to go down and raid the kitchen for a snack, because dinner won't be ready for some time yet.'

'I don't think,' he murmured as he removed the glass from her hands, placing it on a small marble table. 'I really don't think we are talking about the same appetite, somehow.'

'For Heaven's sakes . . .!'

'*Oh Dio,*' he gave a mocking groan. 'You are going to tell me that sunset is not the time to make love . . . that I shall have to wait until after midnight.'

'Well, not really . . .' she grinned sideways at him, her cheeks flushing beneath the gleaming desire in his eyes.

'Not *really* . . .?' he mimicked her words, sliding a strong arm about her waist and brushing a stray hair from her brow before tilting her face up towards his own.

'No, I was . . . er . . . wondering why it was taking you so long to . . . Lorenzo!' she shrieked as with a great shout of laughter he swept her up into his arms.

'Ah, my lovely wife, how I shall miss you when I go to Rome tomorrow.'

'Rome? Tomorrow?' She looked at him with consternation.

'Only for a few days. The time will pass very quickly,' he said as he carried her down the spiral staircase. 'And after all, we do have tonight, *cara.* Hmm?'

The long empty days and nights following Lorenzo's departure seemed to be unending. Due to pressure of business he was forced to extend his stay in Rome and despite the fact that he called her frequently on the telephone, Darcy was tortured by visions of the beautiful women which she knew inhabited the Eternal City.

Business was one thing, but his leisure hours were

quite another, she told herself, gloomily aware as she gazed in the mirror that she was not looking her best. Maybe it was the intense heat of the long hot summer, but during the last few days she had been overtaken by a somnolent lassitude, a drowsy weariness which made even the simplest task almost too much to contemplate.

She had planned to while away the tedious hours until Lorenzo's return with study of the manuscripts in the library, but somehow even the thought of some original historical research failed to excite her interest. She felt so extraordinarily tired all the time that she preferred just to sit by the window of her suite, looking out at the magnificent view, her mind filled to the exclusion of all else with the prospect of Lorenzo's return.

Aunt Paola had begun to fuss at Darcy's pale complexion and her lack of interest in the delicious food placed in front of her.

'Come, child, you must eat. You are not looking well and your husband will be angry when he returns to find you looking like this. He will say we are not caring for you properly.'

'Hah!' Adriana had snorted angrily. 'It will do him no harm to see what a mistake he made, to have married such a one. *Mi fa schifo!* It makes me sick!' she shouted, jumping up from the lunch table and running towards the door. 'Perhaps now he will see how stupid he has been!'

'Oh Dio, Dio.' Both Aunt Paola and Uncle Vito had blanched, fulsomely apologising for their daughter's behaviour.

'I'm sorry she doesn't like me,' Darcy had replied sadly. 'But there's nothing I can do, is there? Let's forget it, please.'

Darcy had repeatedly tried to become friends with the tempestuous girl, all to no avail. Adriana still continued to regard her with loathing and without Lorenzo's protective presence the spiteful pinpricks were beginning to get under Darcy's skin.

There was a knock on the door and she looked up with a smile, expecting to see a maid with the mid-morning cup of coffee. Her mouth dropped open with surprise when she saw that it was Adriana who stood hesitantly in the doorway, her arms full of flowers.

'I ...' the girl hesitated, her cheeks flushed as she stared down at the floor. 'I'm just going to do the flowers in the family chapel and I wondered ... well, I wondered if you would like to come too. Some of the mosaics are rather fine, I believe.'

Darcy looked sceptically at the girl whose eyes were still firmly fixed on the floor. She didn't for one moment believe that Adriana had thought of showing her over the chapel. It was much more likely that it had been Aunt Paola's suggestion. However, at least the girl was being polite and possibly trying to make amends for her behaviour. Besides which, Darcy thought, she'd never seen inside the chapel which had been locked since her arrival, Lorenzo informing her that the key had been lost.

'Yes, I'd like to come with you, it's a kind thought, Adriana,' she said, getting up from her chair and accompanying the girl down the corridor.

'This must be surely the oldest part of the castle?' Darcy looked about her with interest as Adriana fitted the huge iron key into the ornate brass lock, leaning against the heavy oak door and allowing Darcy to precede her into the sunlit chapel.

She stood staring about her, her eyes round with wonder. 'It's ... it's perfectly lovely,' she breathed, gazing at the dazzling red, blue, gold and silver mosaics on the walls which told the story of the Creation and other episodes from the Old and New Testaments.

Darcy went over to run her fingers lightly over the tiny chips of stone, marble and precious metals that had been made up into such lovely scenes so many hundreds of years ago, marvelling at the artistry and expertise of the artist who had constructed such a vision.

'There's something here that might interest you,' Adriana called from a small side chapel. 'Over there,' she pointed to a grey marble plaque on the bare white wall.

In sharp contrast to the other memorials which were either written in Latin or Italian, the one pointed out by Adriana had been clearly chiselled in stark, plain English. Darcy's eyes swept over it, hardly comprehending the words before she turned to stare at Adriana. With dawning horror she registered the girl's flashing, brilliant smile of triumph, the deep hatred in the hot, sultry eyes.

'Well, *cousin!* Your dear husband has made a fool of you—has he not?'

Feeling suddenly sick and breathless, Darcy looked again at the inscription:

ERECTED BY HER SON, LORENZO DI
TANCREDI
IN LOVING MEMORY OF
HELEN TALBOT, LATE OF BELMONT HALL,
ENGLAND
BELOVED WIFE OF EMILIO DI TANCREDI,
CONTE MONTREALE

'It was I who burned for revenge . . .' Lorenzo's words echoed and pounded in her brain as the inscription blurred in front of her eyes, the chapel growing suddenly cold and dark. The last sound she heard as the swirling mists claimed her trembling figure, was Adriana's high, shrill, hysterical laughter.

CHAPTER NINE

DARCY slowly returned to full consciousness, Aunt Paola's worried face swimming into view as she gently swabbed Darcy's forehead with a cool, damp cloth.

'Where ...? I ... I don't understand ...' Looking around her bedroom in bewilderment, she struggled to sit up only to fall back on the pillows with a groan as a sharp pain shot through her head.

'You fell and hit your head on the floor,' Aunt Paola murmured nervously.

'The chapel!' Darcy gasped. With hideous clarity her mind was suddenly filled with the scene. The brilliant, prismatic colours of the mosaics danced before her closed eyelids as she heard Adriana's wild, uncontrolled laughter and saw again the memorial stone, the words of which seemed to be burnt into her brain.

'Oh no! It can't be true—it can't!' Her fingers clutched the older woman's arm feverishly as the dull ache in her head began to throb painfully.

'Hush, child. All will be well, so just lie here quietly until the doctor comes.' Disregarding the evasive, soothing words, Darcy could see the confirmation of the dreadful truth in Aunt Paola's unhappy brown eyes.

'Oh God!' Darcy breathed, closing her eyes as the pounding in her head gained in intensity.

Revenge! Lorenzo's revenge for the treatment of his mother by Darcy's family. That was why he had bought Belmont Hall and why he had insisted on staying married to her. Just for revenge! She couldn't prevent a weak tear from escaping from beneath her closed eyelids as the separate pieces of the jigsaw puzzle which had so preoccupied her thoughts for the past month, all began to neatly slot into place.

Aunt Paola who had been gazing down anxiously at the girl's chalky white face, looked up in relief as a small, plump man carrying a black bag bustled into the room.

Dottore Baldini listened to a stream of Italian from Aunt Paola and then courteously but firmly showed her out of the room before coming over to sit down on the bed.

'Well, Contessa, I hear you fainted and banged your head on a hard marble floor. Yes?' Darcy nodded, wincing as his fingers gently probed the back of her head before thoroughly examining her eyes and reflexes.

'Just a mild concussion,' he pronounced at last. 'I suggest that you rest here for the remainder of the day. You should be fine tomorrow.'

'Thank you. I'm sorry to have been a nuisance.'

'It's no trouble at all. In fact,' he grinned. 'It gives me a chance to practise my English. I did some postgraduate medicine at St Bartholomew's Hospital in London for a year, and enjoyed myself very much in your country. However, this fainting is not good. You are a new wife, I understand. When was your last period?'

'My what . . .' Darcy looked at him in bewilderment, her mind still struggling to comprehend the full extent of Lorenzo's consummate revenge for the way her family, and particularly her father, had rejected his mother.

'I am suggesting that you might be pregnant—that you may be expecting a baby.' The doctor smiled down into her confused blue eyes.

'Oh no. I just had a shock and fainted. That's all. I mean . . .' her voice trailed away as the full import of his words struck her like a blow. She couldn't . . . surely it wasn't possible . . .?

'. . . controllo delle nascite?' the doctor was saying, clicking his teeth irritably as he searched for the correct English. 'Have you been taking precautions against having a baby?' he asked.

'No, I . . . er . . . I never thought . . . I mean . . .'
Darcy's head throbbed as her spinning brain told her
that it was entirely possible and more than likely that
she was indeed pregnant. 'Oh God!' she groaned
helplessly. 'What am I going to do?'

'What you are going to do is to lie here quietly and I
will come and see you again in a few days. There will be
plenty of time to discuss such matters later, so there is
no need to worry yourself about it at the moment, no?'
He stood up to leave.

'No,' she murmured helplessly, her mind still not able
to fully comprehend the second blow she had received
that day. First Lorenzo and now . . . now a baby. It was
all too much for her to cope with. She must have time
to think—she must!

'Please, Dottore,' she caught his hand as he turned to
go, 'I would be grateful if you didn't . . . well, if you
didn't tell anyone about . . . about the baby, please?'

'You will wish to tell your husband first, of course. I
quite understand,' he said, patting her hand. 'I am sure
that Conte Monreale will be delighted to know that he
is to have a son.'

'It is just as likely to be a girl,' she muttered,
wondering what on earth she was doing lying here and
discussing the sex of an unborn child—the very least of
her problems.

'You are quite right, of course,' Dottore Baldini
laughed. 'But my dear Contessa, no prospective Sicilian
father would ever admit to such a thing!'

Left alone, Darcy lay back exhausted as she stared
blindly at the ceiling trying to bring some sort of order
into her chaotic thoughts. She remembered the tension
and the pain in Lorenzo's voice as he had told her
about his mother. The mother who had struggled and
fought to keep his inheritance together until he was old
enough to take the burden off her shoulders. No
wonder that the iron had entered his soul as only
sixteen years of age, he had watched her die.

Despite her own manifold problems, Darcy couldn't prevent a lump forming in her throat and the tears filling her eyes as she thought of the young, lonely boy. She was almost sure, knowing and loving Lorenzo as she did, that it was at that point he had conceived his vengeance—his vendetta against her family.

Why else should he have bought Belmont Hall, a house that would normally have no interest for him? If it hadn't been a desire for revenge, such an attractive man would have never for one moment have thought of marrying Claire or herself. It was now quite clear to her that either of the two sisters would have done, it was just her bad luck that Uncle Henry had made such a mess of the marriage rehearsal.

When was he planning to tell her? Just as soon as they moved back into the refurbished Belmont Hall, no doubt! Darcy ground her teeth with rage, her feelings of frustrated anger and furious outrage taking over from her initial pity for the young Lorenzo. How he must have laughed. How he must have gloated at the success of his scheme to pay her father back for the unkind treatment of his sister—an aunt she had never met.

Oh, my God! Darcy sat bolt upright as she realised that not only was Lorenzo her cousin but that everyone here in this castle was a relative in some way or other. That dreadful girl Adriana had called her 'cousin' in the chapel, which must mean that she knew . . . Of course she did! Darcy cursed herself for being so stupid. They all knew, but it was only Adriana, whose spite and hatred for Darcy had been sufficiently strong to overcome Lorenzo's command for silence. Darcy was sure he had forbidden the family to say anything, he wouldn't want to spoil his little 'surprise', would he?

She gasped as a sudden shaft of pain at Lorenzo's cruel deception seared through her trembling body. What had she, Darcy, ever done to him that he could treat her in this way? Had he planned that she should fall in love with him? He must have. His revenge would be all the sweeter for that, wouldn't it? Every time he made love to her . . . She blushed a deep crimson as she tried not to think how she had moaned and trembled in ecstasy beneath the power of his sophisticated expertise, his mastery of her emotions. What amusement her capitulation must have given him . . .! Darcy writhed in an agony of shameful embarrassment, her slender body suddenly racked by heavy sobs. With a deep groan she buried her head in the pillows, completely unable to prevent the helpless tears of love and longing for her husband. A husband who quite obviously had felt nothing for her, but simply used her as a convenient tool in his long-term plan of revenge.

Falling at last into an exhausted sleep, she was shaken gently awake by Aunt Paola, asking if she would like an English cup of tea. Nodding miserably, she staggered to her bathroom to try and repair the ravages of her storm of weeping.

'The doctor has said that you must rest today, Darcy,' Aunt Paola murmured as she helped the girl back into the bed.

'Yes,' she replied dully, noticing, however, that the older woman had not made any reference to a baby, so the doctor must have kept his word.

There was a long heavy silence between the two women as Aunt Paola busied herself with the tea cups.

'You knew . . . you knew all along that . . . that Lorenzo's mother was my aunt Helen, didn't you?' Darcy said in a quiet voice.

'No, no—not at all!' Aunt Paola protested. 'Believe me, I had no idea that Helena—we always called her Helena, you see—was your aunt. I promise you that, truly!' Darcy looked into the anxious, unhappy eyes of Lorenzo's aunt and saw that she did indeed speak the truth.

'It was when I was showing you the jewellery, you remember the day? It was then that I suddenly realised . . . You mentioned Helena's home, Belmont Hall, and

that your name was Talbot. I . . . I was so surprised and
shocked that I felt ill, surely you remember, Darcy?'
Aunt Paola took heart from the girl's nod. '*Si, si*, it is
true. I tried to speak to Lorenzo that lunchtime—*O
Mama mia*, I saw you looking at Helena's picture and
I was sure that you didn't know and I didn't know
what to do for the best . . .'

'Why didn't Lorenzo allow you to tell me the truth?
Surely he must have given you a reason?'

'No, no. He just said, "I forbid it. She is not to know
until I tell her myself." I could not understand it, Darcy.
It is very nice to find that you are Helena's niece, that
we are all family, *si?*' She shook her head in puzzlement
at her nephew's inexplicable command.

'Adriana doesn't think so.' Darcy's flat statement of
fact hung in the air between them.

'*Che roba! Oh Dio, Dio*, what a mess!' The older
woman sighed unhappily. 'It is all our fault, Vito's and
mine. Please understand, Darcy, it started so innocently.
Just an amusing idea—no more than that.'

'And what amusing idea was that?'

Aunt Paola winced at the hard, sarcastic tone in
Darcy's voice. 'Please! You do not understand. Vito
and I were married soon after Helena and Emilio and
for many, many years I wished to have a baby. I . . . we
. . . we saw the doctors and we prayed but the Good
Lord denied me such a blessing.' She sighed.

'Helena, who had Lorenzo of course, was so sweet, so
kind. She helped me to bear my misfortune. "Never
mind, Paola," she would say. "I am sure that one day
you will have a child, and if it is a girl we must marry
her off to Lorenzo, so we will always be one, big happy
family." It was just a kindness, a little joke to make me
feel better, you understand?'

Darcy nodded reluctantly, suddenly swept by a wish
that she had known her aunt Helen who had obviously
been as kind as she was beautiful.

'And then, when I had completely given up hope, I

found I was pregnant, and we had Adriana. Oh the joy!
I couldn't believe that God had been so good to me.
She was such a lovely baby and Vito and I were so
proud of her. She grew up to be beautiful and we . . .
well, it seemed natural somehow that we should think
of her as Lorenzo's wife to be. It would have made
matters so . . . so comfortable. Lorenzo was the heir to
all this . . .' she gestured about her. 'Surely you can
understand?'

Darcy, looking at Aunt Paola's expression as she
tried to explain, thought she did understand. Poor
Uncle Vito and his wife who, not to put too fine a point
upon it, lived on the charity and goodwill of Lorenzo.
His firm 'behave or get out' speech at dinner their first
night had only emphasised the obvious harsh facts of
life here in the Castello Tancredi. No wonder that it
had seemed a good idea that Adriana should marry
Lorenzo. Being indigent, poor relations was one thing,
being the parents of Lorenzo's wife and the grand-
parents of the future heir to 'all this', was obviously
another.

'So Adriana was brought up to believe that she
would eventually marry Lorenzo?'

'No, no. Her father and I never talked to her about
it, but she must have heard us discussing such a thing,
of course. I promise you Darcy, I had no idea that she
even knew of our . . . our wish, until Lorenzo
telephoned Vito and told him that he was married and
would be visiting us soon.' She sighed heavily.

'Adriana raged and stormed and screamed . . . it was
terrible . . . terrible!' Aunt Paola's face blanched as she
remembered the scene. 'Her father and I tried to reason
with her of course, but with little success.'

'Does she love him very much?' Darcy asked calmly,
as if it were someone else sitting up here in bed
discussing a possible love affair between her husband
and his young cousin.

'No . . . no of course not! What should such a child

know of love?' the older woman protested. 'I think she had just come to think of herself as the future . . .'

'. . . Contessa?' Darcy dryly supplied the missing word as Aunt Paola blushed unhappily.

'*Si, si.* It was her pride that was hurt, you understand?'

Maybe, Darcy mused, but then again, maybe not. A vivid picture of the girl's ripe, sultry beauty flashed before her eyes. Oh yes, Adriana wanted to be mistress of the Castello Tancredi, but she also wanted its *conte*—of that Darcy was quite sure.

'But you must believe me, my dear Darcy. When you arrived, and Vito and I saw how beautiful you were and how much Lorenzo loved you, we could only be happy for him. Truly. You have only been here with us for a short time, but Vito and I have become so fond of you. It is terrible that Adriana should have done such a bad thing . . . to have been so unkind. *Che roba!*'

Che roba! is just about the right expression. 'What a mess' indeed! Darcy thought, seething with frustrated anger as Aunt Paola made her apologetic way from the room. Here am I, married to a man who merely wished to possess me for his own diabolical purposes, and . . . and now I'm expecting a baby! Once again she made some fast mental calculations, falling back with a deep groan on to the pillow. It seemed certain that she was pregnant; what on earth was she going to do?

Exactly the same criteria which had prevented her flight from the apartment in London, applied here in Sicily. She had no friends or relatives on whom she could rely, no one to whom she could turn for help. Only now—matters were in a far worse state. She now knew that, dreadful thought though it was, she was in love with Lorenzo. She ought to hate him for what he had done to her; however, there was no denying the fact that while her mind roundly condemned his behaviour, her body still longed for his touch. Of course, she'd get over that weakness in time, she'd have to, but time was something she didn't have. Lorenzo would soon return from his business trip to Rome, and once he found out about the baby . . .

'I'll never be free of him—*never*!' she cried out loud in an agony of despair. The thought of having to spend the rest of her days tied to a man who not only did not love her, but quite clearly never would, was utterly unbearable.

This is no time for weeping! she angrily told herself as she tried in vain to staunch the tears which obstinately kept flowing down her cheeks. She had to pull herself together and make some plans—fast. She didn't know how she would escape from the castle or where she would go when she did; but somehow she must formulate a plan. If Lorenzo di Tancredi, Conte Montreale thought that his duped wife would be waiting patiently for his return, he was going to have to damn well think again.

What an incredibly hot summer it was, Darcy thought, putting down her book with a heavy sigh and leaning back on the bench to gaze up through the needles of the giant redwood tree at the sun blazing overhead. She'd always loved the botanical gardens, here in Cambridge, and during the last month she had come here most days to either lazily feed the ducks on the round pond, or to sit reading in the shade of the trees. Moreover, since the gardens lay just around the corner from her new small flat in Panton Street, it couldn't be more convenient.

Glancing down at her watch she saw that she ought to be getting back soon to have some lunch before setting off for her afternoon's work. During the nightmare journey back to England, her constant worry had been how she would manage to support herself once she arrived. However, in the event she needn't have worried. Her first, tentative approach to one of the language schools had been crowned with success. They had been suddenly let down by a part-time teacher, and with her good degree in history, she had been welcomed with open arms. Teaching modern European history to foreign students just over in Cambridge for the summer, wasn't exactly what she would have chosen for a career. However, she was grateful for the regular pay cheque which for the present kept her housed and fed.

Darcy had spent a frantic twenty-four hours desperately trying to plan her escape from Sicily and yet, in the end, it had all been so simple. Not able to sleep at night, she had silently roamed the stone corridors of the castle, coming across a black dress and long black woollen shawl in one of the bedrooms. Putting on the dress and wrapping the shawl about her head, she had slipped through a back door at first light and caught the cable car down the mountain. A rickety old bus had taken her to Palermo, from where she had caught the ferry to Naples and a train for the rest of the way back to England.

It had, of course, been the most horrendous journey of her life. Not only had her body been racked by the aching discomfort of the hard seats, but her mind and soul had been tormented by the thought of Lorenzo's betrayal.

Every day of the long, tedious month which had passed since her escape from Sicily had only increased her hopeless love and longing for her husband. Recently, however, the harsh economic facts of life had begun to worry her more and more. Of course she had been to see a doctor as soon as she had arrived in Cambridge, but what she was going to do eventually, especially when the baby arrived, she still hadn't managed to sort out. She certainly had a problem on her hands, as Claire had pointed out when they had met just over two weeks ago.

'For Heaven's sake, Darcy—what a dump! Why did we have to meet here of all places?' Claire had looked down at her British Rail sandwich in disgust. 'Waterloo Station Buffet—madly exciting, I must say!'

'Can it be that sudden family riches have gone to our little blonde head?' Darcy queried with a smile, and for a few minutes it was as if she and Claire were back in their teens as they robustly traded insults with each other, before the laughter stopped and they looked quietly at each other.

'Come on Darcy. Spill the beans—what's up?'

'Have you ... have you heard from Lorenzo at all?' Darcy murmured, not quite able to meet her sister's eyes.

'No, not a cheep. Should I have? I mean, I didn't even know you were back in the country until you phoned.'

Darcy sighed with relief. It wasn't that she didn't trust Claire, but just in case her sister had told anyone where she was going, a London railway station had seemed a suitably anonymous place to meet.

Claire watched quietly while her sister fiddled with her tea spoon. 'You'd better get on and tell me all about it—whatever it is,' she said at last. 'That's why I'm here, isn't it?'

'Yes,' Darcy agreed, with a wry smile. 'The thing is, I don't want you telling Mother most of what I'm going to tell you, just let her know that I'm safe and well—okay?'

'Okay. Now for goodness sake, get on with it. I can't bear the suspense!' Claire laughed.

She wasn't laughing by the time Darcy had finished telling her about their long lost aunt Helen and why Lorenzo had bought Belmont Hall. How he had forced Darcy to stay married to him after the wedding rehearsal which had gone so drastically wrong and why, when she found she was going to have his baby, she had been unable to contemplate a future life with Lorenzo.

'I don't know what I'm going to do about the baby. I'm going to keep it, of course,' Darcy explained. 'However, I haven't worked out exactly how, yet. Still, I expect something will turn up.'

'Cripes! I hope so,' Claire fervently agreed. 'You must make some definite plans soon, really you must. Are you pleased to be having the baby?'

'Yes ... I ...' Darcy blushed in confusion. How could she possibly explain to Claire the extremely complicated feelings she had over the child she was carrying, when she didn't really understand them herself. It was because it was part of Lorenzo, of course, she realised with an unhappy sigh.

'That damn husband of yours has been perfectly foul, hasn't he?' Claire fumed. 'I mean, I can understand him being set on revenge for our father's treatment of his mother—absolutely typical of Father, wasn't it? But honestly, Darcy, that was when he was a young boy of sixteen. He's in his mid-thirties now isn't he? He's rich and he's powerful, he's got all the goodies that life has to offer, what pleasure can it give him to grind our family down into the dust? Although in fact,' she paused, adding slowly, 'he hasn't done that, has he?'

'Done what?'

'Well ...' Claire hesitated, looking at her sister in puzzlement. 'Oh, sure, he's got Belmont Hall and the best of British luck to him, especially if it's a cold winter!' she laughed. 'Seriously though, what's the net result of everything that's happened?'

'Oh, for God's sake! I thought that at least you'd understand,' Darcy snapped irritably.

'I do, and that's half the problem. You say that Lorenzo's got this vendetta against the family, right?'

'Absolutely right!'

'Okay—so what's he achieved? Our parents are living in a super house in absolutely the best part of London; Mother has an annuity which dear Father can't get his hands on and fritter away; and until you bolted from his side, you were covered in jewels and clothes that would cause most women to gnash their teeth with envy. You can call it what you like, Darcy, but I don't think either "revenge" or "vendetta" exactly fit the bill, do you?' she looked quizzically at her sister.

'Besides which,' Claire added. 'It really doesn't tie up with all his kindness to me. I'd never have been able to go over to America and see darling Roddy if it hadn't been for Lorenzo; he really was so sweet and helpful.'

'Hah!' Darcy snorted, before she realised the full import of her sister's words. 'Just exactly how "sweet and helpful" was he, Claire?'

'Well,' it was Claire's turn to blush as she stared down at the table. 'He made me promise not to tell anyone, although I never understood why,' she sighed. 'I didn't have a chance to tell you all about Lorenzo and the sale of the house, did I?'

'No. I've waited a long time to hear all about it,' Darcy replied grimly.

'Well, I met Lorenzo at some boring party. I didn't know anyone and was just wondering how I could manage to disappear when the hostess brought him up to be introduced. I must say that even I could see he was the most attractive man there. All the women in the room were on "full red alert", if you know what I mean?'

Darcy remembered her first evening out with Lorenzo at Langan's Brasserie. 'Yes,' she sighed. 'I know exactly what you mean.'

'Well, he was looking bored to death—can't say I blamed him—until he caught my name. He asked if I lived at Belmont Hall, and when I said that I did, wow! He went straight into overdrive, and I found myself whistled out of the room and sitting down having dinner with him at the Mirabel, no less before I'd managed to catch my breath. I love Roddy very much and Lorenzo really isn't my type, but honestly Darcy, if you could have seen the astonishment on the other women's faces at my having snapped up Lorenzo from beneath their noses . . .! It made my week, it really did!' she laughed.

'Anyway, to cut a long story short, he put his cards on the table straight away. He told me that he was interested in our house, but didn't know how to approach Father. Would I introduce him? I said sure, why not? So he arranged to drive me up next day. After Father had shown him around the house, Lorenzo came and had a quick word with me, specifically about Father's oddball idea of Lorenzo and I getting married. I laughed like a drain—I mean, the whole idea was too silly, wasn't it?'

'Yes, crazy. Lorenzo just managed to shuffle the pack and I got landed with the joker!' Darcy mused sourly.

'Well, this is where things start getting weird, Darcy, so please listen carefully. Lorenzo seemed to think the scheme was as stupid as I did, but in a different way. He was sort of laughing ruefully and swearing with impatience all at the same time. I asked him what was wrong, but I'm not sure he heard me properly. He kept going on about it being the right house but the wrong girl. Anyway, in the end he started oozing Latin charm and so I weakly agreed to say "yes" to Father and to trust Lorenzo to sort out the problem. Father trotted into the room at that point, so we didn't manage to discuss it any further. With me so far?'

'Loud and only too clear.'

'The next thing that happens is that Roddy rings up, and although I tried to be guarded, he wormed the story out of me and had a blue fit. He says I'm not marrying some Italian lothario, I've got to marry him, etc., so I agree like a shot—naturally! Slightly panicking at this point, I ring Lorenzo. A joke's a joke, I tell him, but not if I'm going to lose the man I love. He says, fair enough, come down to London and we'll talk about it.'

'I hope all this has some point, Claire?'

'Just wait. I go along to his scrummy apartment—I know you don't like it but I think you're crazy—and after I've explained about Roddy he picks up a telephone and casually arranges for me to have a first class seat on Concorde to Boston! Now that was kind of him, you can't deny that?'

'No, I can't,' Darcy agreed suddenly wishing that she hadn't decided to talk to Claire. For some extraordinary reason, all this talk about Lorenzo was making her feel quite sick with nerves.

Claire took a sip of tea. 'Well, I'm looking at him with open mouth, etc., and he explains he can't muck up my life just to please himself—what price your revenge theory?—and he hopes that I'll be very happy. I tell him I'm over the moon, but what about his problem viz the right house and the wrong girl? He looked a bit put out there, and said he didn't know he'd told me about Darcy. My mouth really dropped open at this point. I mean, I didn't know that you knew each other, you see.'

'We didn't—of course we didn't!' Darcy burst out angrily.

'Okay—Okay! I'm just telling you what he said. It was all a bit muddled, but from what I could make out he was nuts about you. Anyway, I buzzed off to America, everything was absolutely super and when I return, Lorenzo is at the airport to meet me. All the way back to London he's sort of fizzing with excitement. He tells me that you are both madly in love with each other and are getting married the next day. Fantastic, I say, I'll be there to toast you both in champagne. He then waffles a bit; says it's all rather more complicated than it sounds, and that I'm not to turn up until it's all over—the wedding, I mean. Well . . . I started to get a bit worried at this point, but he told me that I must trust him, he hasn't let me down yet, has he? And honestly, Darcy, I was so grateful to him for fixing my flight to see Roddy, that I could only agree . . .'

Darcy looked at Claire in open-mouthed shock. 'Either one—or both of you—are completely mad! It wasn't a wedding, it was just a rehearsal. Lorenzo knew

that perfectly well—*the swine!* It only went wrong and
we found ourselves married because old Uncle Henry
got his wires crossed as usual . . .'

'. . . Now, that's where you're wrong! Lorenzo told
me quite clearly that he had been to see Uncle Henry
and it was to be a proper wedding. It was only to look
like a rehearsal, he said, because you didn't want a
fuss.' Claire looked earnestly at her sister. 'So you can
see why I was so upset when you told me, after you
were married, that you didn't love Lorenzo.'

'Oh God!' groaned Darcy. 'I don't understand any of
this claptrap, and from what you say it's all far, far
worse than I thought. Why should he have married me
if not for revenge? I could understand him not wanting
to admit the mess that the rehearsal-cum-wedding
landed us in, but not this . . . this deliberate
wickedness!'

'Don't you think you ought to talk things over with
Lorenzo?' Claire asked tentatively. 'He must be worried
sick about you, and you are expecting his baby, after all.'

Darcy glanced at her watch. 'I must go now. I know
you've tried to be helpful, Claire, but I'm afraid that
Lorenzo has told you nothing but a pack of lies from
beginning to end. The thought of him worrying about
me is just one, big laugh. Having set out to accomplish
his crazy revenge, the only worry he'll have, will be how
soon he can get a divorce! As for the baby,' she
instinctively put her arms about her body. 'I . . . we . . .
don't need him. I'd rather die than ask for his help or
assistance.'

'Where can we get in touch with you? You aren't
going to be too proud to let Mother and I do what we
can, are you?' Claire pleaded.

'No—no, of course not.' Darcy smiled wanly at her
sister. 'Don't forget to give my love to Mother. I'll let
you know where I am . . . er . . . eventually,' she had
promised, getting up to kiss her sister before melting
quickly away in the rush-hour crowd.

She really mustn't meet up too often for a talk with Claire, Darcy thought as she gathered up her books and left the botanical gardens. She had been thoroughly upset at talking to her sister about what had happened between her and Lorenzo. So much so, that it had taken her well over a week to get back to some sort of equilibrium. She had hoped that time would cure her of the intense longing for his presence, the aching need for the caress of his hands on her body, but it hadn't happened. The long nights were especially hard to bear. So many times she had fallen into an exhausted sleep in the early hours of the morning, only to wake at dawn to find her cheeks still wet with tears.

Sighing heavily, Darcy walked slowly back up the street towards the large Victorian house which had been converted into flats. Immersed in her unhappy thoughts, she only gave the long black sports car parked outside the building a cursory glance as she turned to mount the steps.

A small warning of alarm seemed to be niggling at the back of her mind as she entered the dimly-lit hall. Frowning, she turned to look back at the car parked beside the pavement; her figure suddenly stiffening in fright at the sound of voices which issued from the open door of her landlady's ground floor flat.

'But I've told you she's out ... And if you want my opinion ...'

'I don't want your opinion. I want my wife—and I am prepared to wait here all day—if necessary!'

Shaking with terror, Darcy dropped her books with a clatter as she whirled to flee back down the steps; the ruthlessly hard, rich dark tones of the well-known voice seeming to echo relentlessly in her brain.

CHAPTER TEN

HELD firmly in the grip of a blind, mindless panic, Darcy's slim figure raced down the street, her ears filled with a sudden roar and squeal of brakes as a long black car slewed across the pavement in front of her, effectively barring her progress.

'Get in, Darcy.'

She stood panting and gasping for breath as Lorenzo leaned over and opened the passenger door. 'Get in—at once!' he commanded harshly.

'No! I . . .' she looked wildly about her for an avenue of escape.

'Mannaggia!' he swore impatiently as he bounded from the car, striding swiftly to sweep her up in his arms and dump her struggling figure unceremoniously on to the seat.

'You—you can't just kidnap me like this!' she shouted in fury as the Ferrari snaked in and out of the mid-day traffic.

Lorenzo gave a short bark of sardonic laughter. 'Can I not? Well it would seem that I have just done so!'

'I'll . . . I'll open the door and . . . and jump out if you don't stop immediately!' she cried.

'If you intend to commit suicide, it's as good a way as any that I know of,' he replied with infuriating calmness as she sat beside him almost weeping with frustration.

'However,' he continued. 'It would be a pity to terminate your existence when I merely wish us to have lunch and talk together quietly. I give you my word that I will drive you back to your flat when we have finished our discussion.'

'The only thing we have to discuss is our divorce!'

'That and other matters,' he agreed with maddening

imperturbability. 'So I suggest, *cara*, that you relax and enjoy the drive, it won't take long.'

She looked out of the window to see that they had reached the outskirts of Cambridge, the supercharged engine responding with a roar as he put his foot hard down on the accelerator.

'Where . . . where are you taking me?' she burst out almost hysterically. 'You can't make me go back to that . . . that ghastly apartment where you used to keep all your women. You can't!'

'Ah . . .' He gave a small sigh, accompanied by a rueful shake of his dark head. 'So that was why you always disliked it so much! I should have guessed, of course.'

Darcy averted her head to stare blindly out of the window. She could feel a deep tide of crimson spreading over her face as the full significance of her question and his reply hit her like a blow to the solar plexus. Was it because she had been jealous of the other women in his life that she had always hated the apartment so much? But that must mean . . . she gulped nervously, that must mean that she was already almost half-way to falling in love with Lorenzo by the time they found themselves married to each other, and . . . and that was ridiculous!

'Where are we going?'

Lorenzo took his eyes from the road momentarily to shoot a penetrating glance at her pale trembling figure. 'I am taking you home, of course. Where else would I take you?'

Home? She glanced up to see a signpost for Newmarket flash past as the sports car roared down the dual carriageway. Belmont Hall—of course. But it wasn't her home any more, was it? With a weary sigh of resignation she lay back in her seat. Lorenzo was right, there was no point in trying to escape. She would just have to grit her teeth and somehow manage to stagger through the afternoon until, as he had promised, he took her back to Cambridge. When they had finished raking over the cold ashes of their disastrous marriage, she would be thankful to regain the peaceful security of her small flat, she told herself, trying to ignore the heavy lump of depression which seemed to have settled in her stomach.

Stealing a glance through her eyelashes at his stern features, the tanned arrogance of his profile as he concentrated on the road before him, Darcy clasped her shaking hands tightly together. Clothed in slim, immaculate beige trousers topped by a short-sleeved cream shirt open at the neck to display the strong column of his throat, Lorenzo's powerful frame exuded such an air of raw, vibrant masculinity that she felt suddenly breathless, her knees trembling violently beneath the skirt of her pale blue cotton dress.

'How ... how did you know where to find me?' she murmured, breaking the long silence which had settled between them.

'I returned from Rome to find the castle in uproar because my wife had disappeared. It only took a few minutes' concentrated thought to know exactly where you were.' She winced at the underlying bitterness in his hard, flat voice.

'Where else would you go, my dear Darcy? What else would you do, but return to your books and your academic studies?' he drawled blandly. 'It only took my investigators two days to track down your address. Simple, no?'

'Yes, I ... I suppose so,' Darcy agreed in a small voice. Very close to tears she turned to gaze out of the window, pretending to take an interest in the swiftly passing scenery. He had known where she was for over a month! And not once, during all that time, had he bothered to contact her or tried to see her. Not that she wanted him to, of course. The whole point of her escape from Sicily had been to get away from him. However, since he had always known where she was and hadn't bothered to do anything about it ... well, it just showed how little he cared for her, didn't it?

The rest of the journey was completed in a strained silence, Darcy being far too miserably absorbed in her painful thoughts to even attempt any conversation. The crunch of car wheels on gravel jerked her out of her gloomy self-absorption and raising her head she saw that they had arrived outside the front door of Belmont Hall.

With legs that felt as if they were made of cotton wool, she allowed Lorenzo to help her out of the car and lead her shaking figure up the broad steps and into the Hall.

Wilkins bustled forward, greeting Darcy with a beaming smile. 'How nice to see you back, madam. I do hope that you enjoyed your holiday and that you had a good rest?'

What holiday? What rest? She flashed a startled glance at Lorenzo, whose cheeks flushed slightly as he briskly ordered that lunch was to be served immediately.

Darcy silently shook her head as Wilkins offered her the bowl of fruit. She had been hardly able to eat any of the delicious food and now, as Wilkins placed the coffee tray on the table before closing the dining room door firmly behind him, she felt quite sick with apprehension.

For a man who very seldom drank any alcohol he was certainly making up for it today, she thought inconsequentially, watching Lorenzo pour himself a large glass of brandy from the decanter which Wilkins had left on the table. She gazed fixedly down at her hands, bracing herself to listen to Lorenzo's plans for their divorce.

It seemed that he was in no hurry to begin the discussion. Sitting back in his chair, slowly rotating the brandy glass between his hands, his dark, heavy-lidded gaze rested speculatively on his wife's lovely face. The silence lengthened between them, becoming almost unbearable as she stole a glance at the indomitable figure sitting at the end of the table.

'Well, Darcy, we must talk, yes?' he said at last in a bland voice. 'Our marriage has in some ways been an unfortunate affair, has it not? It did not start under what one might call ... er ... auspicious circumstances, and you have felt that not only were you blackmailed into remaining with me as my wife, but that all control and direction of your life had been taken away from you, hmm?'

'A masterly summary of the situation!' she grimly agreed.

'This is one side of the coin,' he continued quietly. 'There have been many other aspects of our life together which have been immensely rewarding and very ... er ... enjoyable, have there not? I am, of course, referring to our private, personal life, *cara*.'

'Count Montreale's profit and loss account?' Darcy retorted scornfully, her cheeks flushing as she tried to evade his dark, glittering eyes.

'Ah, my Darcy, I can see that you are still angry— both with me and the situation in which you found yourself. It is understandable,' he added. 'However, I have allowed you a month for calm reflection and thought. Surely during that time you have been able to see matters in their true perspective?'

'Allowed me ...? Hah! You've got a nerve.'

'But yes. I did not arrive on your doorstep breathing fire and demanding that you return to me, did I *cara*?' he murmured sardonically.

'But ... but that was only because you weren't interested one way or another ...'

'*O Dio, Dio!*' he groaned impatiently. 'Can you not give me the credit to have realised that after all you had gone through, you needed time to consider what was best for yourself and our child?'

Darcy's eyes widened in shock. 'You ... you know about the baby?' she gasped.

'You could hardly expect Dottore Baldini not to mention the matter to ... er ... to the father concerned, surely?' Darcy flushed at his bitter, ironic smile. 'The good doctor was worried about your health, but I saw from my agent's weekly report that you had visited a competent physician in Cambridge. I decided, therefore, that there was no need to be alarmed.'

'You ... you bloody man!' she cried, shaking with impotent rage. 'Poking around in my life, putting your snoopers on my trail ... Why in the hell can't you leave me alone?'

'Why do I not leave you alone? *Cristo!*' he groaned, pushing a distracted hand through his black hair as he regarded her with piercing intensity.

'I am reliably informed, Darcy, that you have a first class mind to go with your first class degree. It has never ceased to amaze me, therefore, that you seem to be incapable of any rational thought as far as your own emotions and personal relationships are concerned.'

Darcy flinched at the cold, cutting words and the chill gleam in his hooded eyes.

'It seems that I must put matters succinctly. Despite the unpromising beginning to our marriage, I want you to clearly understand that I do not wish for a divorce. On the contrary, I earnestly hope that we will live here together at Belmont Hall and bring up our children in ...' he paused, '... in peace and harmony. Above all, I must emphatically deny that I married you in a spirit of revenge, or from some extraordinary idea of vengeance. It is a perfectly ridiculous idea, Darcy, which a moment's intelligent thought should have made quite clear.'

He gave a harsh, mocking laugh. 'Oh yes, I talked to Claire—as indeed you knew very well that I would!' He paused to gaze searchingly into her unhappy blue eyes. 'Do you really fear me so much? Am I truly such a monster, Darcy?'

'Oh no! I ... I ...' she shook her head in helpless

distraction at the inability to express her bewildering, confused emotions.

'Let us, however, keep to the point. To put it quite simply, *cara*, you must now decide what it is that you want to do. It is for you to tell me whether you wish to stay married to me or if you intend to leave me permanently and arrange a divorce.'

Darcy looked up in startled dismay as he rose from the table. 'I must now go and see the builder's foreman about some of the outbuildings. I suggest that you take your time to consider the matter very carefully. You might like to look around the house and see if you approve of my alterations. I shall be back for your answer in just over an hour.'

'But ... but you haven't explained *anything*!' she wailed. 'Not why you bought this house, or why you stayed married to me after that ghastly wedding rehearsal or ... or anything ...'

Lorenzo stood looking down at the trembling distraught girl for a long moment, his tanned, handsome features presenting an inscrutable mask.

'No, and I don't think that I intend to, not at the moment,' he said at last, measuring his words slowly and carefully. 'We lived closely together for well over a month before you ... er ... ran away. Surely, if we are to have any kind of future together, that period should have given you ample time to have come to an understanding about the sort of man I am—hmm?'

Darcy shrugged unhappily. He was asking too much. How could she possibly make a decision without all the relevant facts? The only ones she knew at the moment condemned him out of hand.

'You see, *cara*, I have the possibly ridiculous desire to possess a willing wife and not a blackmailed hostage to fortune.' The grim twist to his mouth belied the cynical amusement in his voice.

'During the whole of our ... er ... relationship I have made all the decisions—forced the pace as it were—and that was something which you bitterly resented. So now, today, you are going to make a decision entirely on your own. A relationship is nothing if it is not built on trust. You see, I am going to trust you to make the right choice, and you may trust me when I promise to accept and abide by whatever you decide.'

'You ... you haven't mentioned the baby ...' she whispered, feeling almost numb with misery. 'You don't seem to care about ...'

'*Non tormentarmi!* Don't torment me, Darcy!' Lorenzo's eyes blazed fiercely, the rigid control of his emotions slipping for a moment, before his face became once more a taut, blank mask.

'Shall I tell you about the anguish I shall feel at not being able to see my son grow up? Would it help you to make a reasoned judgment? I think not!' he answered the question bleakly, a vein beating wildly in his temple.

'Lorenzo! I ...' Darcy's deep blue eyes swam with tears while a hard lump seemed to be constricting her throat.

'I must leave.' He ran a surprisingly gentle finger down her pale cheek. 'Just listen to your heart, *carissima*,' he murmured softly, before turning abruptly away, the door clicking quietly behind him.

Darcy sat gazing down at the polished surface of the long oak table as if in a trance. Her mind seemed to be paralysed, resolutely refusing to function as her whole being throbbed for the comfort and security of Lorenzo's strong arms. She simply wasn't capable of the rational thought that he was demanding. How could she make a decision of such overwhelming importance when every fibre of her being was aching for his unobtainable love?

Despite what he seemed to think, she *was* listening to her heart; a heart whose message was one of pain and misery whichever path she chose.

Leave Lorenzo and she faced long lonely years as a single parent, desperately struggling to kill her love as she tried to bring up their child without his help. There would be no financial worries of course, Lorenzo would insist on seeing that his child wanted for nothing. But a child needs more than money, it needed two parents and the security of a loving home. Something she and the baby would have to do without.

Stay with Lorenzo and she faced long lonely years as a wife whose love for her husband was not reciprocated. A wife who was merely one of his possessions to be picked up and then dropped again on the whim of the moment. He would adore his child of course, but what of her? He found her sexually attractive at the moment, but she knew she could never hope to compete with the glamorous, sophisticated women who inhabited his world. When he tired of her body—as without love he must do sooner or later—then what?

Her head throbbed and ached as she tried to resolve her cruel dilemma: The short, sharp surgery of the knife immediately, or a long drawn out, ultimately terminal existence.

With a deep sigh, Darcy rose from her chair, her head still a mass of conflicting emotions. Wandering slowly through the ground floor rooms she was surprised to see how little Belmont Hall had been changed. Lorenzo had obviously installed central heating, although it took her some time to notice the hot air vents let so carefully into the skirting boards of the old walls.

The new raw silk curtains and deep pile carpets were in softer shades than the original colour scheme, while the furniture gleamed as never before. Mrs Wilkins at work no doubt, Darcy thought wryly, as she looked about her at the shining silver and bowls of fresh flowers; so very different from her mother's haphazard housekeeping.

Still shrouded by a heavy pall of miserable indecision, she trailed into the old kitchen, now transformed into an efficient yet at the same time warm, homely room.

The Wilkins had obviously gone back to their cottage, she thought, leaning against the new oil-fired Aga.

''Ullo girl, I didn't know you was back from your holiday. Had a good rest, did you?'

Darcy turned to see James entering the room and easing himself into his jacket which hung on the back of the door.

'His Nibs said you was tired and had gone away for a good rest. I must say you still look a bit peaky to me, Darcy.'

'Oh James, it is good to see you,' Darcy smiled warmly at her old friend. 'How is everything, and ... and are you really happy here with the Wilkins?'

'Yeah, we all get on like a house on fire, and I haven't eaten so well since I don't know when. You wait till you try Mrs Wilkins' apple pie!' He looked around the kitchen.

'Bit of a change, ain't it? My God, Darcy, you'd never credit what it's been like these last six weeks. His Nibs was like a bloody tornado, driving the builders to hurry up and get everything done. They only went yesterday, you know.'

'Yes ... er ... it all looks very ...'

'So it should! What it must have cost doesn't bear thinking about. Been spending money like water, he has. Even got my old cottage fixed up a treat. Well, I tell you, I've never been so comfortable in me whole life.'

James looked at the tall, strangely silent girl. 'I hopes you ain't sour that he gone and done it all without you being here? Because if you are, you shouldn't be. If he asked me once, he asked me a thousand times how you'd like this or that done—fair wore me out it did. Still, you've got a good bloke there, Darcy, and no mistake. I know he looks as hard as old blazes, but I reckon he's a right soft touch as far as you're concerned!'

'No, I'm delighted at how ...'

'Funny how we all thought he was keen on Claire, when it was you he was after all the time. Rum thing, that. Ah, well, I can't stop here gossiping all day, I've got to go and plant up my leeks.'

After he'd gone, Darcy wandered slowly back through the hall and up the wide oak stairs, drawn almost irresistibly towards her old bedroom. Opening the door, she stood looking about her in amazement.

Although her desk was still in front of the window, the wall where the bed had been was now lined with shelves containing her old books, together with those from her Cambridge flat. The comfortable armchairs had been recovered to match the new curtains in a fresh version of the old, original chintz. What had once been a bedroom was now a quiet, welcoming study.

Moving over to the desk she looked down at its contents almost unable to believe her eyes. There, on the leather topped surface, were the old and very valuable parchment manuscripts which had so excited her interest in Sicily.

He ... he must have brought them over from the Castello Tancredi for ... for me! she thought, gazing in wonder at what was for her—apart from his love—the most precious gift that Lorenzo could bestow.

Gazing sightlessly out of the open window, her mind was suddenly filled with flickering images: Lorenzo's abrupt dismissal of Susie when she had been rude to Darcy in the restaurant; his care and concern for her mother's comfort and his kindness to Claire. She saw through fresh eyes his insistence in Sicily on the 'respect' which he felt she merited; his need to know that she and the baby had been well and healthy in Cambridge and his recognition, shown by his re-arrangement of this room, that she could not exist without academic work of some kind.

He might not love her—maybe such a controlled, hard man was not capable of love as she understood it—but there could be no denying the fact that what he had to give, he had unreservedly placed at her feet.

As if in a trance, she got up and slowly left the room, wandering down the wide corridor and glancing at bedrooms which seemed to have been transformed from the draughty, uncomfortable places that she remembered. Her dazed mind was still trying to assimilate her reassessment of Lorenzo, when she opened the door of what had once been an old box room, and which now seemed to be a lobby leading into a suite of rooms warmly lit by the afternoon sun.

Passing a sumptuous bathroom and a dressing room with one of his suits on a hanger, she entered through an arch into a large room dominated by a huge four-poster bed, hung with pale blue, raw silk drapes. Her feet sinking into the thick cream carpet, she walked slowly over towards a small object lying on one side of the bed.

The emotional trauma of the whole exhausting day suddenly proved too much for Darcy as she bent down to pick up her old teddy 'Threadbear'. Clasping him in her shaking arms she threw herself across the bed, quite unable to stop the tears from flowing down her cheeks.

She had no idea how long she lay weeping silently, her body racked by deep sobs, before she heard a harsh exclamation and strong arms enfolded her trembling figure.

'*Ah, non piangere, gioia mia!*' Lorenzo murmured soothingly as he gathered her into his warm embrace. '*Su, non piangere*, my precious darling. Come, do not cry.'

'Oh, Lorenzo . . .' she sobbed. 'I . . . I've been such a fool!'

'No, no my darling. It is I who . . .' he sighed, gently wiping the tears from her eyes before covering her upturned face with butterfly-light kisses.

'Yes, yes I have,' Darcy sniffed, her body still being shaken by occasional sobs. 'I . . . I . . . Oh Lorenzo, I can't leave you. You've b-been so g-good to me, and ... and anyway, I ... I love you far too much!' she whispered, burying her face in his shoulder.

'Ah ...' Darcy felt the breath being expelled slowly from his powerful body in a long drawn out, emotional sigh. 'At last!' he murmured thickly, his arms tightening about the slender figure nestling in his embrace.

'My darling, *ti amo, ti amo* my lovely Darcy. *Cuore mio* ... My heart's desire, I have been in such torment!' he groaned huskily. 'I think that the gamble I took today must have been the most dangerous one of my whole life!' He gave a shaky laugh before crushing her fiercely to him, his mouth descending to cover her quivering lips in a kiss of demanding, hungry possession.

'Gamble ...? I ... I don't understand ...' Darcy murmured in confusion as she lay dazed in his arms some moments later.

'My darling idiot! Did it never occur to you that I arranged to marry you and I insisted on staying married to you, quite simply because I was hopelessly in love with you?' He sighed at the incomprehension in her deep blue eyes.

'Darcy, I must admit that when I was young, I was consumed with a desire for revenge against your father. However, when I grew up and became involved in my own business affairs, it was not something about which I thought a great deal. You must believe me!'

'Yes, I ...'

'*Va bene*. Now, my darling, your father who is no business man kept selling off his land—parts of the original family estate—to pay his debts to the bank. I had obviously been interested in my English relations and had made enquiries about them. As each piece of land came on the market, I bought it. Not for vengeance, you understand, but to retain what was part of my own blood inheritance. Why should a pension fund or an insurance company buy and farm the land that once belonged to our common ancestors, Darcy? I felt that it was quite wrong and besides,' he grinned, 'I must tell you that land is an excellent long-term investment!'

Darcy looked at him in amazement. 'Do you mean to say that you own all the land Father sold?'

'Most of it, yes.' He smiled. 'So you can see why buying this house made sense, hmm? However, I was often away on business and so I left the matter in the hands of my agents, who sent me regular reports of land bought, and *ipso facto*, the sorry tale of your father's progression down the financial ladder.'

'I . . . I can see why you bought the land, but . . . but how could you have fallen in love with me? We'd never met before Claire's engagement party.'

'With . . . er . . . excessive zeal, one of my investigators included some photographs of the family with his regular reports. I did not take much notice at first, you understand. And then I found myself, almost without conscious reason, asking for more and more pictures of a tall, gangly, blonde student.' He paused as Darcy shook with amusement.

'Ah no, *cara*. Ah no—you mustn't laugh . . .'

'But darling—it's too silly. You can't possibly have fallen in love with . . . with a photograph!'

'Well, I . . . er . . . I bought a computer business in Cambridge which I found needed a great deal of my personal attention, and therefore I did manage to . . . er . . . catch glimpses of you as you went about your daily life.' He grinned sheepishly as she let forth a peal of laughter.

'Stop laughing—you witch! I told myself at the time that I was a crazy fool,' he sighed. '*Matto da legare*— stark, staring mad in fact! But you had wormed your way, God knows how, so completely into my heart that when I received reports that you were seeing a great deal of your clever boyfriend, Richard Petrie, I became quite desperate.'

Darcy slipped loving fingers through his silver-tipped black hair. 'Darling, why didn't you just knock on my door and say "hello"—or something?'

'Say "hello"?' He snorted derisively. 'My God—how English! Darling girl, can't you understand that I had to possess you *totally*. And therein lay my problem because there was nothing I had that you were likely to want. I knew instinctively that money, as such, simply wouldn't interest you. My title? You would have just laughed. I couldn't pay court to you in the normal way because our lives were too separate. Besides, I wasn't an academic and you were far too involved with your studies to be interested in any other kind of man.'

'Oh, my God—what an intellectual snob you make me sound!'

'No, my love. But without some form of study, you are not happy.' He gently brushed a stray lock of hair from her brow. 'When we were in Sicily, I finally understood that I could not fight such a compulsion. I realised that if I continued to deny you the books you needed, I . . . I would lose you for ever.'

Darcy suddenly remembered Lorenzo's desperate lovemaking after he had found her in the library of the Castello Tancredi. Caused, she now saw, by his overwhelming need to reassert and prove his domination of her body. She shook her head in dazed wonder. 'I . . . I still can't take it all in. I mean, I was just a very ordinary student . . .'

'Oh no, my dearest—you were delightful. Even in those dreadful horn-rimmed spectacles, not to mention the rubber bands in your hair—*Oh Dio!*' He shook with laughter.

'Pig! Still, if you cared for me when I looked like that, I suppose it must be true—that you love me, I mean.'

'*Se ti amo? Certo che ti amo—certo, certo!*' he murmured thickly, his fingers moving to undo the buttons on her dress. 'When we made love, how could you not have known? Surely you must have realised just how much I adore you?'

'For Heaven's sake . . .' she protested weakly as his hands moved softly over the burgeoning fullness of her breasts. 'You . . . you still haven't explained how . . .'

'We can talk later! Just now I must . . .' Lorenzo's powerful frame shook with barely suppressed passion as his soft caresses became more insistent, more possessive. 'Do not deny me, my sweet one. It has been so long, yes?'

His hoarse whisper sent shivers tingling down her spine. The rampant desire in his dark, smouldering eyes caused her heart to beat a rapid tattoo. 'Oh, Lorenzo, I love you so much,' she breathed, before the searing touch of his lips ignited a flame deep inside her and she rapidly began to lose all sense of time and place. The only true reality seemed to be the hard warmth of his tanned body, the quivering ecstasy engendered by his sensually arousing mouth and hands as they moved erotically over her soft flesh.

'*Oh Dio . . . Dio . . .!*' Darcy barely heard the low, deep groans forced from his throat by the sheer wanton abandonment of her response. Great waves of passion shook and overwhelmed her, crying out with joy as at last he brought them both to an earth-shattering climax.

'I've never had a bath with a man before,' Darcy mused languidly as Lorenzo gently soaped her back.

'Ah, what a loose woman you have become,' he mocked. 'Making love in the afternoon, and now lying here in the water beside your husband—such depravity! When I think what a sweet, innocent virgin you were when we first met,' he shook his head sorrowfully. 'It's very, very sad!'

'Oh, poof!' Darcy grinned as she blew a soap bubble in his direction. 'Actually, I wasn't nearly as strait-laced as you seem to think. For instance, I assumed that you

and Claire were lovers . . . well, you had got engaged to
her. And from the way you behaved towards me,' she
added darkly, 'can you wonder at it?'

'Ah, *cara* . . .'

'Ah, *cara*—nothing! Don't you try and wriggle out of
it—you behaved disgracefully!'

'Yes, I did, didn't I?' He gave a rumble of laughter.
'But my darling, surely even you can see the delicious
irony of the whole affair? Claire has told me that she
has related to you how she and I met, and how she
agreed to be "engaged" to me, yes?'

'Well, I must admit that I thought it was all a pack of
lies. However, it was truly kind of you to send her off to
America to see Roddy.'

'Why not?' He turned over in the water to bestow a
long, lingering kiss on her softly parted lips. 'Unfortunately, I became so involved with my business take-over
that I forgot to phone your father and call off the deal.
So, when he telephoned to invite me to the engagement
party, I felt obliged to go through with the evening,
planning to sort it out when Claire and I had managed
to talk together.'

'But darling, Claire was still in America, and Mother
and I were nearly out of our minds with worry,' she
recollected with a shudder.

'Yes, but at the time I assumed she had returned. So I
bought her a ring as a small consolation present for all
the trouble I had given her, and drove up to Suffolk.'

'She . . . she didn't choose the ring . . .?'

'Ah, no—another small lie, I'm afraid. But as soon as
I realised that you weren't Claire and that there was
only one other person you could be, I had to improvise
fast!' He laughed happily. 'Can you blame me, my
darling, for making hay while that particular sun shone?
To have the girl I loved in my arms at last? It was surely
asking too much to expect me to behave like a
gentleman!'

'I was terrified of you. I kept trying to warn Mother

and Father, and then you started kissing me out on the terrace, not to mention that ... that dance! Really, it was quite awful!'

'Awful? Are you going to have the nerve to look me straight in the eye and tell me that you found my kisses "awful"?'

'Yes—absolutely frightful!' she retorted, trying to keep a straight face.

'Minx!' he growled, pulling her soft body close to his own. 'Just let me show you how awful and frightful I can be!'

'Lorenzo—for Heaven's sake!' Darcy giggled, her cheeks flushed as she struggled to sit up some moments later. 'I think I'd better put some cold water in this bath if you're going to behave like *that*!'

'Ah my dear love, *cuore mio*—my heart's desire ...' he murmured huskily. 'No amount of cold water will ever cure my ardour for your sweet body.'

'Oh, Lorenzo!' Darcy's eyes shone radiantly at the man she loved so much. 'I must say that is the most utterly romantic thing I've ever heard! But ...' she frowned suddenly. 'We only met once before that awful wedding. I mean, you might have *thought* you loved me, but you didn't know, not really?'

'I was sure before we married and totally, absolutely certain the day afterwards! I am a very ... er ... physical man, *cara*. Your passionate response to my lovemaking was so enchanting and so much more wonderful than I could ever have dreamed possible, that I ...' He laughed. 'Oh, my Darcy, how I love to see you blush!'

Laughingly trying to evade the water she splashed in his direction, Lorenzo stepped out of the bath and returned with a large white towel. 'There is no doubt, however, that we owe all our happiness to your great-uncle Henry. When you had the inspired idea of a rehearsal, I suddenly saw how all my problems could be resolved.'

'Did you . . . did you really arrange with him that it should be a real wedding?' she asked, colouring slightly as he helped her out of the large bath and began to dry the moisture from her body.

'Yes. I told him such a tale of true love thwarted, that even I nearly cried!' Lorenzo grinned. 'Although you, my dearest, nearly blew the whole ceremony. *O Dio!* I could see you getting ready to stop the service; thank goodness those horrid children distracted your attention. I still tremble when I think what a close shave it was.'

'I . . . I felt it was so wrong, somehow. Not . . . not fair to you.'

'I know, *cara.*' His voice thickened as he gently swabbed her firm breasts. 'You always hated that wedding. I think that we will ask your local vicar to marry us again, properly this time. Would you like that, hmm?'

'Oh yes,' she breathed, looking up at him with shining eyes. 'Then I will feel properly married.'

'I will arrange it as soon as possible,' he promised.

'We haven't really talked . . . I mean, are you . . . er . . . pleased about the baby?' she asked in a small voice.

'Oh, my darling, can you doubt it?' He gathered her gently into his arms. 'You are going to have my son— *Dio*, I am a very lucky and fortunate man. When Dottore Baldini told me, I . . . I broke down, *cara*. I've never been so unhappy in my whole life—*never!*' His dark eyes were shadowed with pain.

'But darling, why, oh why didn't you tell me about your mother and . . . and our family connection. It . . . it was such a terrible shock when Adriana . . .'

'That stupid little girl!' Lorenzo ground his teeth angrily. 'I shook the truth out of her and she is now being despatched to a very strict Swiss school, where I fondly hope that she will be very unhappy! Really Darcy, the idea of my marrying her was too ridiculous—I don't even like the girl! No . . .' he added, his firm lips cutting short her protest with a hard, determined kiss. 'No, she must be taught some discipline. She hurt you and I cannot have that.'

Lorenzo led her slowly back into the bedroom. 'Why did I not tell you about my mother? My sweet one, by the time I had the opportunity, when we were living in the apartment in London, it was far too late. How could I tell you then? Our relationship was so fragile, and there were so many heart-stopping moments when I feared I had pushed you too hard. I tried to keep you so busy that you would have no time to think, but I was always frightened that you would simply run away. As indeed you did in the end,' he added sadly.

'It wasn't until we had arrived at the castle that I remembered the memorial stone in the chapel. I quickly arranged to lose the key and hoped for the best. *O Dio!*' he groaned. 'I can hardly bear to look back over the last month. There were so many times when I nearly got in the car to drive to Cambridge and beg you to come back to me. But I had to leave you in peace, and hope against hope that whatever you felt for me, it would surmount all the problems we had encountered in the past.'

'Oh Lorenzo!' Darcy slid her arms around his tall figure, pressing herself closely to his body. 'Everything is all right now. We have each other and . . . and the baby. We're so lucky! Although . . .' she paused, smiling up into his gleaming dark eyes. 'It does seem only fair to point out—as Dottore Baldini will tell you—that you may well be having a daughter and not a son!'

'No—really?' A slow smile spread over his tanned face as he gazed down at his lovely wife. 'I'm very glad you pointed that out, *cara*, I wonder why I didn't think of that before? We must obviously practise the art of producing sons, and therefore I suggest that we begin immediately!' He laughed, sweeping her up into his arms and carrying her over to the bed.

'Again? But you can't . . . I mean . . . Lorenzo! *For Heaven's sake . . .!*'

Coming Next Month in Harlequin Presents!

783 TROPICAL EDEN Kerry Allyne
Against her wishes, a powerful development company bids on her father's resort. And despite her engagement, she's drawn to the arrogant usurper of her tropical Eden.

784 THE FIRE AND THE ICE Vanessa James
Two years after penning a scathing article about a wealthy playboy-editor, a reporter runs hot and cold when she finds herself working for the man behind the myth.

785 THE ONLY ONE Penny Jordan
For the rags-to-riches chairman of Hart Industries, the previous owner of his fifteenth-century estate is elusively appealing, fleetingly desirable at any price.

786 THE PASSIONATE LOVER Carole Mortimer
An English heiress finds herself stranded in a Montana blizzard then rescued—not by her concerned fiancé—but by his arrogant, presumptuous cousin.

787 THE DAUGHTER OF NIGHT Jeneth Murrey
A London hairdresser traces her natural mother to ask for help with her foster parent's medical bills, only to be accused of blackmail and subjected to a masterpiece of extortion, involving marriage!

788 TOTAL SURRENDER Margaret Pargeter
An interior designer's boss might not desert her at the altar the way her fiancé did. But she's afraid if she surrenders to his determined seduction, he'll leave her alone and devastated.

789 NO GENTLE PERSUASION Kay Thorpe
Desperation drives a daughter to plead her father's case with a man she suspects will respond to no gentle persuasion. So she confronts him with a shockingly blunt proposition....

790 CAPE OF MISFORTUNE Yvonne Whittal
Dissatisfied with life in Durban, a teacher becomes the governess at a tropical villa still reeling from the mystery surrounding the death of her employer's wife.

EYE OF THE STORM

MAURA SEGER

A powerful
portrayal of
the events of
World War II in the
Pacific, *Eye of the Storm* is a riveting story of how love
triumphs over hatred. Aboard a ship steaming toward
Corregidor, Army Lt. Maggie Lawrence meets Marine Sgt.
Anthony Gargano. Despite military regulations against frater-
nization, they resolve to face together whatever lies ahead....
A searing novel by the author named by *Romantic Times* as
1984's Most Versatile Romance Author.